CHRISTMAS ANGEL HOPE

Morris Fenris

Christmas Angel Hope
Three Christmas Angels Book Two

Copyright 2019 Morris Fenris, Changing Culture
Publications

Table of Contents

Prologue

Guardian Angel School

Heaven

"Hallelujah! Amen!"

The sound of the voices faded away, as everyone paused, serene smiles upon their faces.

"Very nice. Let's all take a few moments to ourselves before the celebration starts. Polish your halos. Fluff your wings. Practice your smiles." The choirmaster smiled at them before leaving the room.

Hope faked a smile for the choirmaster, as she and her two companions left the choir hall, but smiling was the last thing she felt like doing. She had a problem, and so far, she hadn't been able to come up with anything that might fix it. The loss of the Christmas spirit. Not hers, but her charge's.

"Let's go in here," Charity pointed to the schoolroom.

Hope joined her and Joy. All three of them were part of the Guardian Angel Training School, and all three were on probation for various infractions. As for Hope, she'd failed miserably at helping her last charge and was grateful to be given another chance to get things right. She'd been looking forward to this assignment, loving Christmas and just knowing she was going to be successful, only...her third charge wanted nothing to do with celebrating.

Hope sat down at the small table and dropped her head into her hands. The situation felt hopeless, but that word wasn't even in the guardian angel vocabulary. It just didn't exist in the Heavenly realms, which meant there had to be a solution.

I'm supposed to be inspiring and encouraging my human charge to have faith. It's my job to convince them to keep going, to

5

MORRIS FENRIS

not give up, and to find some way of dragging them from their despairing circumstance. But, if they won't even try and nothing about Christmas seems to move them, then what?

"What are you three angels doing? The celebration is about to begin," Matthias asked, startling all three angels. Matthias was in charge of training the newer guardian angels. He was the one who had to approve of how they dealt with their charges. Hope watched him enter the small schoolroom, stopping a few feet away from their table and towering over them. Hope looked at her friends. When none of them offered an answer to his question, he crossed his arms over his chest and made a noise to let them know his patience wasn't everlasting.

He cleared his throat to gain their attention and then met their eyes, one by one. "Well?"

"My little boy is so sad," Joy told him, tossing her hands out to her sides dramatically.

Matthias nodded in acknowledgement of her response and then looked to the next angel. "And you, Hope? The last time we talked you were excited about your current assignment."

"My charge doesn't even want to celebrate Christmas this year," Hope stated, huffing out a breath, as she dropped her chin back into her cupped hands. "How can anyone not want to celebrate Christmas? It's not...well, it's just not right. Or human. They love Christmas and their made-up celebratory figures. The snowman who danced and sang..."

"...and then melted when the sun came out," Matthias told her with a small smile.

"I'm talking about before that. And humans love the story of the little reindeer whose nose glowed and could fly. That story had a happy ending."

"But the idea behind Christmas has nothing to do with those

things," Matthias reminded her needlessly.

"I know that," Hope nodded, "but in my charges file, she loved all those things until a year ago. Now, she abhors the very idea of Christmas. I'm trying not to hold that against her, but I must confess; it's very hard. Christmas is the most wonderful time of the year, but my charge hates it."

"Well, at least your charge doesn't visit the cemetery every day. It's really sad to watch her cry, day after day, and not even try to get on with living her life," Charity added. Charity was the most mature of the angels in training and had already successfully completed two of the three required special assignments. If she was successful in helping her current charge overcome a soul-searing grief, she would be graduating come the end of January.

Hope and Joy still had to successfully help their first charge before they could even think about helping their second. At this point, Hope would find herself being reassigned to another duty that didn't include interacting with the humans below. That thought made her sad and more determined than ever to find a solution to her current charge's problem; if she only knew exactly what that problem was.

Matthias looked at each of the three and then shook his head. "So you three are just going to sit around up here moaning about your difficult situations rather than try to find a solution to them?"

Joy looked up at him, "What are we supposed to do? I mean, it's only a few weeks before Christmas. How are people supposed to remember they're celebrating the birth of Christ if they are so unhappy?"

Matthias grinned. "You find a way to make them happy. Help them remember the good things in life and give them hope. Hope is what Christmas is all about. Your job is to try to get your charges to see that. You have to remember that a guardian angel doesn't just keep their charge from getting run over as they cross the street; you also have to help your charge in the emotional, spiritual, and mental realm."

The three angels looked at each other. Their expressions slowly started to change. Hope was the first to speak up, as a new idea formed.

"I could help Claire want to celebrate Christmas."

"And I could help Maddie find another outlet for her grief," added Charity. "What about you, Joy? Why is your little boy so sad?"

"My little boy doesn't want his mama to be so sad. She's lonely, and he wants to help her but doesn't know how."

"Maybe she needs a puppy to love?" Hope suggested with a smile.

"Puppies are nice. So are kittens," Charity offered. "An abundance of both are always at the animal shelters this time of year. Maybe your little charge's mother could adopt a new pet?"

Matthias squatted down so that he was eye-level with the littlest of the three angels. "You'll find a way. I have faith in you."

"Thanks?" Joy queried, wishing she had as much faith in herself as the head of the angel school seemed to have. "Maybe we should brainstorm some more ideas."

Matthias shook his head, "That is not going to happen while I'm around. I'm still recovering from the last brainstorming session you three had together. If you need to bounce ideas off of someone, I am always available to you."

Hope exchanged glances with Joy and Charity, all of them feeling embarrassed over their previous failures.

Joy was the first to speak up. "I guess I should probably get back down there, huh?"

"That would be a good place to start," Matthias agreed with a nod and a warm smile. "You should all be busy trying to help your charges right now. Christmas is only two weeks away, and you all should know better than anyone just how fast time can fly. Go and tend to your charges. Remember that I am always here if you need advice or just to talk through a plan."

Hope, Charity and Joy nodded dutifully. "Thank you."

Matthias smiled at each of them. "Off with you all now. Go enjoy the celebration for a bit and then take that enthusiasm back to your duties. We'll have even more to celebrate once you three have your charges sorted out."

Hope silently agreed with her friends. A renewed sense of purpose stirred inside her. Claire was going to rediscover the joy of Christmas whether she wanted to or not.

I just have to remember to comply with the rules and regulations for interactions with my human charges.

Last year, she'd crossed not one, but several lines. As a result, she'd had to explain herself before the head of the Guardian Angel Program. She never wanted to repeat that experience again. Ever.

Joy smiled, "I'm heading down there right now. Thanks, Matthias."

"What about the celebration?" Hope asked her, glancing out the window of the schoolroom to see the other angels gathering around the center of the courtyard. The choir performance was about to start. "We're going to sing soon."

Joy shook her head, smiling brightly as she replied, "There's so much to be thankful for and happy about this time of year. I don't need a celebration to remind me of that. I just need to figure out how to make Sam's dream come true, and everything will work out just fine."

Matthias smiled approvingly at her. "Good luck to you, Joy. I look forward to hearing a good report from you. Charity and Hope, good luck to you as well. The miracles of Christmas are just beginning."

Hope and Charity nodded and then headed across the yard to where the chorus was taking their places. Hope intended to get back to the task of helping Claire. First, she needed just a little added Christmas cheer to help her on her way. Matthias had mentioned the miracles of Christmas, and Hope was most definitely going to need one of those if she was to get Claire's situation fixed before December 25th.

"Alright, is everyone ready?" the choirmaster smiled. When everyone nodded, he lifted his hands and brought them down, as the sound of angelic praises filled the heavenly skies.

"Gloria. In excelsis deo. Gloria. In excelsis deo."

Hope was smiling broadly, as she headed down to check on Claire an hour later. She was brimming with Christmas spirit and couldn't wait to find a way to share that with her charge. Miracles came in many packages; Hope just needed to find out what shape Claire's was going to take.

Chapter 1

Two weeks before Christmas,

Chicago, Illinois

Claire St. Peters hated snow. She hated icy slush that splashed on the back of her jeans when she walked down the sidewalk. She hated the bitterly cold wind that felt like shards of ice in her nostrils when she took a deep breath. She most especially hated the Christmas decorations and Christmas music that seemed to permeate the very air and fabric of the city this time of year.

She'd mistakenly thought that moving to a big city would help her avoid all of the holiday trappings, but she'd been wrong. The city of Chicago seemed filled to the brim with holiday cheer that they wanted everyone to share. The streetlights were even adorned with red bows and pine boughs. She'd anticipated the department store she worked for would go overboard with the decorations on the show floor, but she'd hoped the customer service department would be a little more neutral. She'd gotten half of her wish; the head of the customer service department had left it up to each individual employee to decorate their cubicles to their liking. Claire had abstained from any and all decorations. The first year she'd been asked numerous times if she celebrated Hanukkah. She'd replied that she wasn't Jewish. Those same co-workers had been diligently trying to crack the puzzle of why she didn't celebrate Christmas ever since.

To make matters worse, her apartment superintendent—Marybeth Carlson—was crazy for the holiday and had personally decorated every square inch of the common spaces. Claire couldn't even leave her apartment without being accosted by a smiling Santa standing by the mailboxes, or Frosty the Snowman telling her to have a good day as she left the building.

When Marybeth had insisted that she at least put a wreath on her door, Claire had politely refused, only to return home from work one evening to see that one had been provided and hung for her. There was also a note reminding her that it was her duty to maintain the atmosphere of the hallways, and a wreath upon every door was what was required. Claire had reasoned that, since she didn't actually have to look at the wreath, it was battle she preferred not to fight. She'd thanked a smiling Marybeth the next morning for her thoughtfulness and had promised to return the wreath just as soon as Christmas was over.

She crossed the last street, keeping her head tucked as the wind whipped up and wishing Spring would arrive sooner than later. "I should have gone to Florida. Maybe then I could have ignored the holidays. After all, palm trees and sandy beaches are about as far Christmas as one can get."

She looked up, as she finished talking to herself. She'd spoken much louder than she'd intended and had drawn the curious glances of several people standing nearby. She gave them a tight smile and headed for the employees doors at the side of the building. At least she didn't have to enter through the elaborately decorated department store with their display windows, Salvation Army bell ringers, and smiling employees wishing everyone a "Happy Holiday". It was too much.

"Hey, Claire, wait up," a friendly and familiar voice called from behind her.

Claire rolled her eyes and forced a smile before she turned and waited for Alex to catch up to her.

Alex Singleton stopped a few feet away from her, rubbing his hands vigorously and blowing into them before he grinned at her. "I've lost my gloves again. Brrr. It's really cold outside today. I wonder if we're going to get more snow."

Oh, I hope not.

Claire kept her opinion to herself. These last few years, she'd gone to great lengths to not let others know how much she hated winter and the holidays. Normally, she was able to keep to herself and didn't have to worry about making chit-chat with her co-workers. All that changed this year with the new ownership of the corporation and their commitment to building team relations.

Ugh! Don't they know that some people abhor the idea of someone else getting all up into their business and being nosy?

"So, are you going to the company Christmas party?" Alex asked, as they waited for the elevator to arrive.

"No." Claire didn't elaborate.

"Are you going out of town, then?" he inquired.

"No." Her one-word answers seemed to invite Alex to probe further, so she added, "I usually just stay home for the holiday."

"Does your family live here then?"

"I don't have any family. It's just me," Claire told him, as the elevator doors opened. They boarded it along with several others from their department.

"That sounds depressing. Hey, I have an idea. Why don't we go to the Christmas party together?"

Claire stepped back, hoping to put enough room between them so Alex would quit his mission to involve her in the holiday.

"So? What do you think?"

"I think I probably won't go to the Christmas party, just like I haven't gone to the last three."

Obviously shocked, Alex lowered his voice, "Don't tell me you have something against Christmas."

"Okay, I won't." The elevator doors opened. Claire pushed past several people to exit quickly, tossing over her shoulder, "Nice seeing you. Have a good day."

"Claire..."

She ignored him and ducked into the women's bathroom where she locked herself in a stall and waited long enough for Alex to vacate the area. After five minutes, she left the stall, washed her hands, and ran a comb through her long blonde tresses. Then she headed straight for her cubicle.

The fifth floor of the building housed the customer services division of the department store. They handled everything from credit card payments to online sales. This time of year, they were busier than ever. She started her computer, clocked in, and spent the next four-and-a-half hours dealing with one customer after another.

At lunch break, she headed toward the employee's lounge, but chipmunks singing about Christmastime being upon them changed her mind. She turned toward the elevator, but Alex was standing near it. That avenue of escape became impossible as well. Lucky for her, he hadn't seen her yet. She quickly turned around and walked the opposite direction. The stairwell was to her left, so she pushed through the door but, instead of going down, she went up.

The building was six stories tall, which was modest by Chicago standards, but it was a historic building and many improvements had been made to it over the last few years. The one Claire appreciated the most was the addition of a large greenhouse on the rooftop. Inside there were several walkways, lined by stone walls that contained flowering shrubs and bushes. Large trees, placed in giant pots, and green spaces had been added using a synthetic turf that never browned and didn't need watered.

Patio furniture of all types had been placed throughout the space, allowing for groups of many sizes to congregate for either work or a brief respite. Claire and others used the space frequently as a place to eat their lunch and just unwind from the job's stress and chaos. The walls were sturdy glass panels. In several places, the glass was clear which gave a glimpse of the city beyond. The roof had electric panels that could be opened to allow fresh air in and out, but they remained closed this time of year. It was a nice eighty degrees inside and never dropped below sixty-five degrees in the evening.

She was only slightly out of breath when she reached the rooftop entrance, but she took a moment to calm her breathing before she pushed open the door and entered the greenspace. A pair of miniature orange trees greeted her. She paused for a moment to admire their waxy green leaves and the small white flowers that would soon turn into delicate citrus fruits. With no natural pollinators, a team of gardeners had been hired to manage the space, including the self-pollination of the various flowers and trees.

She nodded at several other employees who were taking advantage of the peaceful area, then she walked toward the back and found a small table that looked out over the city skyline.

Behind her, rising up like a sentry over the other skyscrapers, lie the Shedd Aquarium and the Sears Tower. To her left was the new Trump International Hotel and Tower. To her right lie the beautiful Lake Michigan.

She liked being near the water much better in the summer and fall, but now was pretty amazing as well. All of the small sailing vessels had been dry-docked for the winter. The surface of the lake was covered with broken shards of ice, that slowly moved along its surface. Many thought it looked chaotic. Claire found it pleasing to see so many broken pieces, knowing that just a little rise in temperature would melt all of them to become part of the lake once again.

She sighed and dug her tuna sandwich from her bag and

started eating. She only had a thirty-minute lunch break, and she'd already wasted five of those minutes taking in the view. She stared out the window as she chewed, trying her best to just blank her mind and not think about what was going on around her. She had almost succeeded when a childish voice right next to her jolted her back to the present. She looked down into the eyes of a small child.

"Hi. Do you wanna play ball with me?" the child was gazing at her with anticipation of an affirmative answer. He held out a miniature version of a soccer ball with a ready smile on his lips.

Claire felt the color drain from her face, as she gazed into the child's blue eyes; so filled with trust, and so sure that she had all of the answers. Claire's hands started trembling. Suddenly, she couldn't breathe. She raised one hand to her throat while pushing back her chair to get away from the image of the child which she'd thought had been relegated to her nightmares.

"Lady," the little boy called out, but Claire was in a full-panic mode. She couldn't find her voice. She had to get away. She felt tears fall down her cheeks, but she didn't even bother to wipe them away. She grabbed her lunch bag, stuffed the remainder of her sandwich inside and then reached for her purse. The strap had caught on the far side of the table and try as she might, she couldn't get it free.

Half crouched out of her chair, she was straining to free the strap and stay as far away from the child while crying and breathing way too fast. Then, a masculine voice entered her nightmare.

"Hey! Are you okay? Here, let me help you." A large hand reached for the strap, instantly freeing it and sending Claire plummeting back down in her chair. She was painfully aware that she was now being scrutinized by two sets of eyes. She gasped for breath, telling herself she was over-reacting, but her mind wasn't listening.

"Hey! Really, are you okay? Are you choking or something?" the man asked, squatting down and peering into her face with concern in his eyes.

"I'm...I'm...fine," she stammered out. "I need to go," she told no one, holding her lunch bag and purse close to her chest. She stood and backed away from them, taking the long way around the table in the process. Once she reached the walkway, she ducked her head and walked as fast as she could toward the exit.

"Wait!" the man called after her.

"Daddy, what's wrong with that lady? All I did was say 'Hi,' and asked her if she wanted to play with me," the child's voice followed her, as she entered the stairwell and began descending the five flights of stairs back to her office.

All he did was say "Hi" and you acted like you'd seen a ghost. He's just a little boy, not... He wanted someone to play with him, and you just acted like a crazy lady.

Claire mentally chastened herself all the way down the stairs, wiping her tears away and trying to get control of her emotions. She was almost successful and took an extra minute to sit on the stairs outside the third-floor doorway to take some deep calming breaths. She closed her eyes, and then immediately opened them when the first thing she saw was the blue eyes of Daniel...No! Not Daniel. Some other child who looked so much like him...

Claire stood up, shaking her head to rid herself of the bad memories and marched back to her cubicle.

It wasn't Daniel. Lots of little boys look similar at that age. Your mind is playing tricks on you. Get a grip, Claire. Maybe if I immerse myself in work for the rest of the afternoon I can forget again. I need to forget again. I can't ...

"Claire, hi. I was hoping to catch you before you went to lunch," Becky Chavez poked her head around the corner of the

17

cubicle.

Claire forced a smile as she turned to greet her new visitor. "I went up to the rooftop. Was there something you needed?"

"No. I just wanted to see if you'd met the new CEO."

"The new CEO? I thought Mrs. Hammerstein's grandson was taking over the department store chain."

"He is, but he's decided to make Chicago the anchor store for all of the others. He just moved here, and I heard he was wandering around the building today."

Claire shrugged, "Well, I doubt the customer service department will be on his list of places to visit."

"I hear he's really dreamy to look at and single as well," Becky told her.

Claire pursed her lips and shook her head, "And I thought I heard that you got married last month. Did I not come to your wedding?"

Becky giggled, "You were my maid of honor, so of course I got married. I was thinking that it's been like, well…never, since you've gone on a date…"

"Don't even go there," Claire told her, the smile falling from her face. "I don't date. Period."

Becky's smile faltered a moment, and then she brightened. "Well, there's a first time for everything. The day is only half over. See you later."

There was a first time, many years ago. Losing half of your heart hurts too badly to ever risk losing the other half. I'm better at being single.

Claire turned back to her computer and sent up a silent prayer. When her phone rang, she eagerly answered it, glad for something else to concentrate on. Today hadn't started out all that great and the middle had been a complete disaster; all she could hope was that her journey home this evening would prove to be the best part of the day.

***

Hope hovered over Claire's desk, realizing that there was something about Claire's past she'd missed or forgotten to look into. Claire had been terrified of Tyler, one of the most adorable little boys Hope had ever seen.

Why would a lovely young woman be terrified of a small boy? Humans are the most confusing creatures.

She stayed with Claire for a few more minutes, wanting to make sure she wasn't going to break down again, and then she headed back up to Heaven and went straight to the schoolroom in search of Matthias. He had some explaining to do or some investigative work to perform. Hope needed to know what had happened to Claire that had provoked such a strong reaction to a small child. Maybe with that knowledge, she could figure out how to get Claire to love Christmas again.

Chapter 2

Travis Hammerstein stared after the young woman, debating about going after her, or just chalking their meeting up to a disaster and letting it go. He looked down when a small hand tugged on his pant leg and scooped up his son, Tyler. "You okay, buddy?"

"Why did the lady run off? She was crying. Was she sad?"

Terrified was more like it. Since when does a child terrify the former director of a preschool? Something doesn't add up. Why is someone with Claire St. Peters' credentials playing customer service rep in my department store.

Travis had just been named the CEO for the Hammerstein Co.'s chain of department stores. They currently had eighty stores across the nation, with another ten slated to be built in the coming two years. The company was thriving in a day and age where many Americans were turning to the Internet for their shopping needs. Travis intended to blend that online shopping experience with a more personal one encountered when visiting one of their stores and taking the company to the top of the food chain. He was well on his way and had earned the trust of his grandmother and his parents in the process.

As an only child, Travis had learned all about the family business at an early age. Rather than resenting those experiences, he'd paid attention. At the age of thirty, he was one of the youngest CEO's in this field. If things had been different, he would have taken the reins two years earlier, but life had thrown him a curveball he was just now learning how to deal with.

Travis had married his high school sweetheart, Emily, right after graduating from college with his business degree. He'd immediately started working on his master's when Emily had found out they were expecting their first child. Travis had been over the moon, and with the financial backing of his family, he'd completed his degree before Tyler had been born, not knowing that Tyler's birth would be the beginning of the end for he and Emily.

Shortly after Tyler's birth, Emily began to get sick. After months of tests and treatments, her team of doctors began looking for a more serious cause to her illness. What they found was devastating; Emily had a rare form of blood cancer that no one had thought to look for because it was so rare. There was only one way to positively confirm a person had the disease. It also had no known cure. It spread to every area of her body in a matter of weeks.

Tyler was only eighteen months old when his mother passed away, and Travis was left trying to cope with his grief at the same time he was learning to be a single parent to a toddler who didn't understand why his mommy was no longer around to comfort him. Those first few weeks, Travis had cried as much as Tyler. Over time, they had both healed and grown closer to one another.

Then, Travis's grandfather had passed away, and his own parents had declined to step in and take over the company. That left only Travis. He readily accepted. But not many CEO's of large corporations were also the sole caregiver for a four-year old. Travis intended to make sure he left his mark on the way companies operated, starting by creating an onsite childcare center in every store across the country. The Chicago store would serve as the pilot study; the lessons learned over the next three months would help guide the introduction of childcare centers in all of the other stores when they held their annual corporate meeting in April.

That was where Claire came in. Amy in Human Resources had been thrilled with the idea of being able to bring her two-year old twins to work with her and had pointed out that they had a very qualified preschool director already on staff. After reading her resume and doing a small background check on Claire, Travis had become convinced that she was the right person for the job. He

21

hadn't gotten too personal with her background information, just enough to find out that she'd run a very successful school. Everyone had been sad when she'd moved away.

She still had a valid state license. The now-director of the preschool had assured him he wouldn't find anyone better qualified than Claire to help him get his new project off the ground. However, after seeing how she reacted to Tyler, he was now second guessing his thought process.

In answer to his son's question, Travis looked at Tyler and shook his head. "I don't know why she was upset, but I think I should go check it out. Don't you?"

Tyler nodded sagely. "You always make me feel better. Can you make the lady feel better, too?"

Travis touched his son's nose and smiled. "I'll give it my best try. How would you like to play with Amy for a while?"

Tyler nodded and then struggled until Travis put him down. "She's got cool toys in her closet."

"I know. She also has some really cool kids."

"Can I play with them?"

"Well, not today, but soon." Travis took Tyler's hand and, fifteen minutes later, he'd deposited a happy little boy in the director of Human Resources' office. He also briefly described his meeting with Claire. Amy looked concerned.

"I should go check in with her," Amy offered.

"Let me. I'm not sure if Tyler upset her, or if she was already upset when he approached her, but her reaction was rather extreme."

Amy nodded. "She's pretty closed off about her past. Several people in her department have stated that she likes to be alone and never joins in on any extracurricular activities. She does her shift and then disappears."

22

"Noted. I'll be back within the hour or have Douglas come up and get him." Douglas was his chauffer and his best friend. He was also Tyler's godfather, and a man Travis had come to count on almost as much as his own father. He'd been with Travis since he'd first graduated from college and had been the rock on which Travis had leaned during some of the darkest weeks and months of his life.

Travis took the elevator down to the third floor and then entered the customer service department. He took in the Christmas décor and the bustling atmosphere of too many problems and not enough time before Christmas to solve them. The tension in the air was almost palpable. Yet, the employees he observed, as he walked toward the office in the corner, all seemed to be handling their perspective calls with professionalism and a degree of calm that he found surprising. He heard laughter, and it seemed that everyone was doing their best to be accommodating and friendly; just as he'd discussed with the management team. He wanted Hammerstein's to become the definition of the modern department store where customer service was everything.

He kept his eyes peeled for Claire, frowning a bit as he reached the back corner and still hadn't seen her. He also hadn't seen any empty cubicles. He knocked on the open door of Steele Warner, the current head of this store's customer service department.

"Got a minute?" Travis asked, inviting himself into the man's office and shaking his hand. Steele stood up and hastily straightened his shirt and tie.

"Mr. Hammerstein…"

"Call me Travis. Mr. Hammerstein was my grandfather or my father, and I'm not feeling nearly old enough to compare myself to them right now."

"Certainly, sir. Please, have a seat."

"Thank you. It looks like everyone is being kept very busy."

"That they are. We had to put on a few more people for the second shift due to the influx of calls coming in. This is the first year where the store has offered Early Bird pricing to online shoppers. While the numbers aren't in, I dare say it is going to be banner year."

"That's what we're all hoping for," Travis nodded. "I actually came down here looking for Claire St. Peters."

"Claire? My goodness, is there a problem? I have to say, she's one of the best employees I've ever had down here. Always on time, never complains when asked to work an extra shift, and her name never comes up in the employee lounge."

"No, she's not in any trouble," Travis hurried to assure him. "In fact, I would like to speak with her about a job opportunity. I realize you will hate to lose such a good employee, but Miss St. Peters has a specific skill set and the experience to take the entire corporation to the next level in the benefits we can offer our employees."

"Really?" Steele looked intrigued. "Are you at liberty to share what this opportunity might be?"

"Of course," Travis informed him. He briefly outlined his plans to start childcare centers in each store, beginning with the flagship store right here in Chicago. "The center will be open to both male and female parents. It will be offered at a mere dollar per hour, and available for all scheduled staffing hours."

"Sir, I don't have to tell you what a benefit that would be to many of our employees. Several of our customer service reps have had to alter their work schedules because their childcare providers have changed their hours. With traffic, they need at least thirty minutes to get to the other side of the city. If they could simply take the elevator to another floor to retrieve their children, it would solve so many problems."

"That's what I believe as well. Now, I was wondering if you could direct me to Miss St. Peters area?"

"Of course. If you like, I'd be happy to ask her to join you in here?" Steele offered.

"That would be very much appreciated." Given the way she'd run from him and his son earlier, he didn't anticipate she was going to willingly agree to meet with him. He turned and gestured for Steele to go about his errand.

"Good, I'll be right back." Steele hurried around his desk and left the small office, leaving Travis to watch him. Steele walked to the far corridor and stopped at the fourth desk from the end of the row. After a brief conversation, Claire stood up and followed him back to his office. The look on her face told Travis she was preparing herself for bad news.

Steele arrived back at his office with Claire and then gestured for her to enter. Looking up and seeing Travis caused the color to drain from her face again. She took one stumbling step backwards but was stopped by the presence of her supervisor directly behind her.

"Mr. Hammerstein, this is Clair St. Peters." Steele made the introductions through the doorway.

Travis nodded, "We've met, albeit, only briefly." Travis took a step back and watched as Claire gingerly entered the office. She looked as if she was preparing to face a firing squad. Once she was several feet inside the office, Travis turned his attention back to the manager. When Steele didn't leave the office, Travis invited the man to do so. "I'm sure you can find plenty of other duties to keep you occupied."

"Of course. I'll be back in ten minutes?" Steele stammered, backing out of his own office with a slight bow of his head.

"Make it an hour," Travis replied, his eyes barely leaving the nervous woman in front of him. Her blonde hair was neatly confined at the nape of her head. At first glance, it didn't appear that she was wearing—or in need of—makeup. Travis had become accustomed to the famous women with whom he associated, all for the media's sake. They had been enthralled with his private life in recent months. It was annoying and not something he felt inclined to tolerate much longer.

"Please, come and sit down."

"What's this about?" Claire asked, not moving from her stance a foot inside the office.

"Miss St. Peters, my name is Travis Hammerstein, and I have something I'd like to speak with you about. Please?" He gestured toward the sitting area in the corner of the office.

Travis hated the fear lurking in her eyes. He disliked the sadness he saw there even more. Claire St. Peters was a gorgeous blonde with grey eyes that should be full of laughter and happiness, and a complexion that begged for the touch of the sun. She was too pale, too thin, and too skittish. Travis wanted to know why and had an unfathomable urge to try and fix whatever was wrong in her life.

He wasn't normally affected so easily by another person's obvious suffering. Yet, with Claire, he had the strongest urge to wrap his arms around her and promise to fight the demons for her. He didn't yet know what those demons were, but it didn't seem to matter. Travis wanted to save her.

He walked over and stood next to one of the large chairs. His upbringing refusing to let him sit before she did. When he simply looked at her, she finally took one hesitant step and then another to reach the opposite chair and sink into it. Then she dropped her eyes and worried her hands in her lap at the same time.

"Claire? May I call you by your first name?" Travis inquired softly. At her slight nod, he smiled, but she didn't see it. Her eyes seemed to be fixed on the carpet. He refused to give up. "You've worked here for several years now, I understand?"

"Yes," she nodded. "Almost four years now."

"And do you like working here?"

"Yes."

"I should tell you that Amy in Human Resources is the one who brought you to my attention. As you've probably been told, I have assumed control of the corporation and will be making some changes for the betterment of our employees and customers, I hope.

"One of those changes involves a new benefit for our employees. I would like to offer an onsite childcare center in each store."

He watched Claire's shoulders tighten, and her fingers grip one another. Her knuckles turned white. He frowned and then asked, "That bothers you?"

She shook her head and then he watched her intentionally relax her fingers before she responded. "It's a good idea. It will give the company another leg up on the competition."

"I'm glad to hear you say that because I would like you to head up the first one here at this store."

Claire's head jerked up, and she shook her head. Her grey eyes looked so wounded that Travis could almost feel her pain.

"No! I can't. I won't." She stood and, without another word, she left the office with steps just shy of a slow run.

"Claire?" Travis called, following her to the doorway. Then he remained silent, so that her fellow employees didn't become involved in something that didn't include them. He watched her walk past the elevator, going to the stairwell and exiting the floor.

Travis narrowed his eyes and followed her, wondering if she was headed back up to the rooftop greenspace. This time in the afternoon, she would be the only one up there, and that was fine with him. Whatever was bothering her needed to be aired, so they could move forward. His intuition told him they didn't need an audience for whatever she needed to say.

He headed for the stairwell, nodding to several employees on his way and giving Claire plenty of time to feel as if she was safe and had escaped his questions and pursuit. He glanced at his watch and then placed a call to his driver.

"Douglas, Tyler is up in Human Resources. I'm going to be a while. Would you take Tyler home and hang out with him until I get there?"

"Sure thing. Want me to feed him dinner as well?"

"That would be wonderful. I don't know how long I'll be."

"No worries. The kiddo and I will grab a pizza and watch the game."

"Sounds good. Thanks."

"Take care of business. I've got Tyler and everything else."

Travis ended the call before he opened the door to the greenspace. He quickly scanned the tables and then walked down the center aisle, frowning when he didn't see his target anywhere. When he reached the end of the enclosure, he heard the snick of the door opening and turned just in time to see Claire slipping back into the stairwell.

She knew I was here and waited until I was too far away to stop her from leaving. What is she running from, besides me? And why?

Chapter 3

Guardian Angel School

Hope arrived in the schoolroom and then made a sound of frustration. She was looking for Matthias. So far, she hadn't been able to find him anywhere. "Where is he?"

"Young angel, who are you looking for?" a deep voice called from behind her.

Hope turned around and then immediately lowered her eyes. "Sir, I was looking for Matthias."

She kept her eyes downcast, trying to find a way to extricate herself from this situation so that she could continue her search. Theo had been the angel in charge of her last year when she'd failed so miserably. He'd been forced to reach out for additional help. That was where she'd first met Matthias, but seeing Theo reminded her of her failure the year before.

"Little angel, you seem to be out of sorts," Theo commented softly.

Hope didn't say anything, not wanting to share her problems with the angel she'd already disappointed. She fidgeted and then she hazarded a glance up, "Do you happen to know where Matthias is?"

Theo nodded and then gave her a thoughtful look before asking, "You're not considering breaking the rules again, are you?"

Hope immediately shook her head and looked him in the eye, "No, sir. I learned my lesson last year." She made the sign of the angel promise, making circles with her thumbs and forefingers and then hooking them together.

Theo smiled and nodded, "That's very good to hear. You'll find Matthias in the music room."

"Thank you," Hope told him, turning to leave quickly, but stopping when she heard her name called.

"Yes?" she halfway turned around.

"Whatever problem you're currently having, talk to Matthias about it and I'm sure he can help you find a solution."

Hope nodded, "I will." She vacated the schoolroom and headed directly for the music room. She found Matthias talking with several other angels who, once they saw her, smiled at him and then left the room.

"Hope? You were looking for me?" Matthias asked.

She nodded and then launched into a lengthy explanation about everything that had occurred with Claire. "I thought she was just being difficult about the holidays. I didn't realize she had a valid reason for hating this time of year so much. Now, I'm not sure what to do. I should have helped her deal with her pain before I tried to fix Christmas for her."

"Fix Christmas for her?" Matthias queried.

Hope nodded and then her shoulders and wings sagged, "I messed up again, didn't I?"

"Well, that depends. Exactly what did you do?" Matthias asked

"Her new boss wants to start a daycare center. What better way to find the joy of Christmas than through the eyes of a child? I saw that Claire used to work with small children and made sure her new boss learned of this. Now he wants her to take over the daycare center project. I didn't realize that being around children—or any child, for that matter—was going to be so painful for her. I didn't do enough homework. Now, a situation I created is causing her great pain."

"Ah," Matthias murmured. "Come and sit down. Let's talk

30

about Claire and her pain."

Hope followed Matthias to a row of chairs and sat, feeling very sad for her charge and regretful for having skipped the discovery part of learning about Claire.

"First, Claire does have a tremendous amount of pain and grief that she needs to deal with. It's been four years and she has just been going through the motions of life and not really living. Forcing her to confront her past and deal with those emotions is going to be very difficult, but if she gives it a chance, she will find that time has softened the hurt. As for her irrational behavior when she saw Tyler…"

Hope gave Matthias a puzzled look, "How do you know their names and so much about them?"

"I have been watching everything from up here." Matthias paused and then lowered his chin and met her gaze as he added, "I also did my homework."

"Oh!"

"Yes, well, as for her reaction to Tyler…he looks very much like her little boy did when he died. I think that, when she first saw Tyler, she thought she was seeing a ghost, not a real little boy. It scared her and then her emotions took over. She's not had time to process everything. She will. Claire is very strong, or she wouldn't have survived this long."

"So, what do I do?" Hope asked.

"Continue on your current course of action. I realize Travis is not your charge right now, but I believe I am going to make that so. He has his own hurts to overcome, and I believe you will benefit from helping both Claire and Travis conquer them."

Hope frowned. "You're giving me another assignment? Plus, Claire?"

"Don't worry, they work well together. I have faith in you. Have a little in yourself."

"I'll try." Silence settled over the room while Matthias just looked at her. Finally, Hope realized he was waiting for her to speak again. "So, I guess I should go check on Claire. She was running away the last time I saw her."

"I believe that would be a very wise decision."

Hope nodded and then left the music room. She headed down to earth, her heart dropping when she arrived at Claire's apartment and saw the young woman lying on her bed, sobbing her heart out while she held a picture to her chest.

What have I done and how do I fix this?

***

Claire hadn't cried this hard since shortly after the funeral. When she'd fled from the greenspace, she'd known she was acting like a coward in avoiding Travis but seeing the little boy earlier had gutted her. She needed time to get herself back under control. Her only problem seemed to be that her self-control had gone missing.

She'd fled the department store, hopping into the first cab she came across, regardless of the cost associated with using that mode of transportation instead of the transit system. She'd been crying and a taxi seemed the most efficient way of getting back to her apartment before she completely broke down. Parking inside the city was so expensive, Claire rarely drove the car that was parked in her space at the apartment complex. That meant relying on public transportation, which had been hard at first, but now it seemed to just be part of her daily life. She'd made it to her apartment, not sure how she'd opened the door since her eyes had been filled with tears. Thankfully, she hadn't passed anyone in the lobby or in the hallway.

Once inside, she secured the deadbolt and chain and then kicked off her shoes, as she headed for her bedroom and the picture

32

she kept on the bedside table. The faces of the two people she'd lost smiled at her. The eyes of the youngest were so like the little boy earlier today. It was uncanny. She touched their faces, wishing with all of her heart she could turn back time.

She held the picture to her chest and let her tears fall, as she tried to turn off the events of four years ago. It had been Christmas Eve, and her husband had arrived home early in the afternoon from his banking job. Scott had been her everything through high school. There had never been any question about whether or not they would end up married and with a family of their own one day. It had been inevitable and had felt like a storybook.

Claire had gone to the local community college and gotten a degree in Early Childhood Education while Scott had taken business courses, then he'd landed a job at the local bank. Their lives were almost perfect. When they'd found out they were expecting a baby, everything had been perfect. Daniel was the most awesome little boy. Claire had delighted each day in watching him grow and learn.

He'd just turned four a few weeks earlier, and Scott had come home with a promise to take him shopping for mommy and a special Christmas present. Claire had a special present of her own she had intended to share with Scott later that evening, and she'd relished a few hours to finish wrapping everything by herself. She'd sent them both off with a kiss and a promise to Daniel to have cookies ready for Santa when he got home.

She'd set the frozen cookie dough out on the counter to thaw and then started wrapping the final stash of gifts, singing along to Christmas carols on the radio and thinking her life couldn't ever get any better. She hadn't known how quickly her life could turn into a nightmare which she would never escape.

Three hours later, the gifts were wrapped, including her special surprise for Scott. Freshly baked cookies were cooling on the counter when the doorbell had rung. If she could turn back time, she would have never left the kitchen and answered the door. But she had.

Two uniformed police officers had been standing with their hats in their hands and sorrow on their faces. She'd gone to school with both of them. The implication of their visit had taken the strength right out of her legs. She'd collapsed to the hard tile in the entry way and listened while they quietly told her there had been an incident at the mall. Scott and Daniel were among those caught in it. They were sorry to inform her that Scott had died at the scene, but Daniel was being flown to the children's hospital some eighty miles away. They were there to drive her to join him.

They had grabbed her coat, located her purse and turned off the radio and the Christmas lights. They'd bundled her into the back of their car. With police lights flashing, they'd taken her on a trip to see her baby. Claire had forced that her husband was dead to the back of her mind. She couldn't deal with that while Daniel was clinging to life.

They'd arrived at the hospital just as the doctors were taking him into surgery. She'd sobbed over his pale body which was hooked up to so many machines and cables. They'd had to physically pull her away from the gurney so the doctors could head into the surgery ward. The police officers had stayed with her for the next eight hours. The doctors had managed to repair some of the damage to Daniel's little body, but they couldn't even be cautiously optimistic about his survival chances. The bullet that had ripped through his little chest had nicked several organs, including his heart and part of his aorta.

They'd placed him in a medically induced coma, so his body could have a chance to heal without him waking up. Any sudden movements could undo their attempts to mend where he'd been shot. Claire had stayed by his bedside, refusing to sleep or eat, for three long days. The nurses brought her fluids, forcing her after the first day to either drink the meal replacements or be removed from the room for her own safety.

She'd consumed them, never letting go of Daniel's hand or taking her eyes from his face. The doctors came several times a day. Each day, their expressions grew grimmer. Daniel's body wasn't healing; his heart had sustained too much damage. His only hope was a heart transplant. A transplant they were hesitant to even request because they weren't sure he could withstand such a lengthy surgery in his present condition.

While the doctors debated the correct path to take, God had seen fit to take the decision from their hands. Daniel had died, despite the extraordinary measures that were being taken to keep his body functioning. Claire had known the minute it happened; she'd felt his spirit leave. A block of ice had settled over her, paralyzing her for many minutes.

He'd been hooked up to so many machines. Even now, she could remember the sound of the various alarms blaring from them. The nurses and doctors had sprung into action, calling for medicines and such to try to get his heart beating again. Claire had fought them all off. Daniel had suffered so much, and she couldn't bear to see them abuse his lifeless body one more time. She'd waved them all away, standing guard over his bed until the nurses and doctors had silenced the machines and the lead doctor had quietly declared the time of her baby's death.

They'd left her there in the room with his body. Claire couldn't have said exactly how long it had taken for the reality of what had just occurred to settle over her. At the time, she hadn't even felt like she had inhabited her body. For a short time, she was frozen. Her mind was too overwhelmed to even fully process what had happened in the last few days. It was a short-term reprieve from what was to come.

When the ice shattered, so did her soul. She had collapsed on the floor, crying so hysterically that the doctors had been forced to administer a sedative to her and admit her as a patient. The special surprise she'd planned to share with Scott was no longer a surprise. Whether it was due to her grief or the stress of losing everyone she loved, the baby she had been expecting died.

She'd only been six weeks pregnant at the time. The doctors and nurses had been as kind and compassionate as they could be, given the circumstances, when she'd started hemorrhaging and suffered a miscarriage. It had been the final straw to her fragile mind. Claire had lapsed into silence but, on the inside, she was screaming.

She'd remained in the hospital for three days before she'd finally convinced them she could deal with the days ahead. The two police officers were still at the hospital, having taken personal leave to stay with her and offer their support. She would be forever grateful to Jim Akens and Marie Michaels. They'd been fellow classmates, but what they had done for her went way beyond their oath 'to serve and protect'.

They had driven her back home and even helped arrange the double funeral for Scott and Daniel. The local minister of the church that her family had attended faithfully presided over it. Reverend Smythe had done his best, but Claire had already retreated within her mind by the time she returned to her hometown. On the surface, she went through the motions, nodding at the appropriate time and appearing to be in control of herself. In reality, she was barely holding onto her sanity by a thin thread.

The day of the funeral had been overcast. It had started to snow just as the coffin was lowered into the ground. Claire had decided to have Scott and Daniel buried together, somehow comforting herself that it was better for both of them. Her rational mind knew they no longer inhabited their bodies and were in a much better place. She couldn't get past seeing their bodies; they'd just looked like they were sleeping.

The next few weeks had been torture. Marie had offered to move in with her, but Claire couldn't stand to be in her own home. After returning from the hospital, she was unable to walk through the house and see the constant reminders of everything she'd lost, so she'd taken to sleeping in the attic apartment. When Marie realized how bad things were, she'd taken Claire home with her. Claire had proceeded to sleep for the next three weeks.

Her assistant director at the preschool had competently managed the business. After a month of grieving, Claire had forced herself to try and get back to what remained of her life. She'd tried going to work, but had hidden out in her office, unable to look at the children or hear the happy sounds of their voices at play without hearing Daniel amongst them.

At first, she'd returned home, but the Christmas decorations, gifts, and even the cookies for Santa were still where she'd left them. She'd been unable to fathom touching any of it, so she had packed up a few of her belongings and arranged for a realtor to come in and sell the house. She hired a cleaning service to dispose of all of the furniture and the Christmas items. She didn't care what happened to them, as long as she never had to see them again.

She moved into a local hotel for the time being and offered to sell the preschool business to her assistant manager. Everyone tried to convince her that she was making a mistake, but Claire was fixed on leaving Indiana. Her parents had both passed away right after she graduated from high school, and Scott had been a late-in-life child. His mother, Clara, was still living, but she suffered from late-term Alzheimer's and didn't recognize anyone. She had been moved to an Alzheimer's facility almost an hour away the year before.

Claire had stopped by to see her a month after the funeral, but Claire's presence seemed to agitate her greatly. After a brief discussion with the medical staff at the facility, it was suggested that she call before coming to visit so that they could prevent future stress on Clara's already strained mind. Claire had agreed to do so, unable to handle any more emotions herself.

Once the house sold, she cashed out all of their bank accounts and used Scott's life insurance money to move to Chicago. She mentally put her past life in a box which she never intended to open again. She had stopped by the Alzheimer's facility on her way out of town to observe Clara through a window. Her mother-in-law wasn't having a good day, so the nursing staff had kindly asked Claire to visit another time. She'd left her information. Three months after moving to Chicago, she'd received a phone call letting her know that Clara has passed peacefully during the night. Scott had already set up plans for his mother's body to be cremated, and her ashes interned next to her husband at the columbarium, making a trip back completely unnecessary. Claire had asked that any of her personal items be donated to a local charity. When she'd hung up the phone, she'd put the final capstone on that part of her life.

Or so she'd thought. Mr. Travis Hammerstein had just opened up the door to a world where all it held for Claire was pain and sorrow. Even though years had passed, she still didn't feel capable of dealing with any of it. She briefly thought about quitting her job and finding another one, but after she calmed down, she realized Travis had only brought to light things she should have already moved past.

The sad truth of the matter was that her husband and son had died. The small part of Scott that remained had been lost a few days later, leaving Claire all alone in the world. No extended family. Even her close friends had been cutoff because they were constant reminders of the life she'd just lost. Now, four years later, she was faced with having to finally deal with everything. She only hoped it didn't destroy her.

Chapter 4

The next afternoon…

Travis stepped off the elevator onto the third floor and turned to his left, intending to catch Claire at her cubicle and insist that she accompany him upstairs to his office. They needed to talk without having thirty sets of eyes and ears watching them. The customer service area was one part of the building where privacy was simply not available. Even the director of the department wasn't able to assure himself of privacy. He had an office in the back corner, overlooking the city. Travis had spent time the day before speaking with Amy and Steele to come up with answers. They'd reached very few theories as to what had triggered Claire's unusual response both to seeing his son Tyler and being asked to head up the new childcare center.

Neither Amy nor Steele, her direct supervisor these last four years, had been able to offer anything of value. It seemed that Claire was an enigma that no one had truly been able to solve. She rarely was seen interacting with other employees in the breakroom. Aside from Alex Singleton, another customer service representative who appeared to have a small crush on Claire, no one who was casually interviewed had any outside interaction with her. She did her job, did it very well, and then went…well, everyone assumed she went home alone.

Travis had always been one for finding a problem and then solving it. This time, he hadn't had to go looking for a problem. It had dropped into his lap. He wasn't sure what tragedy in Claire's past was fueling her fear of him, but he intended to find out and then help her deal with it. A damsel in distress had always been his Achilles' heel. The fact that he was attracted to this particular damsel only made him that much more determined to put a smile

39

upon her face and wipe the tears and sorrow from her eyes. Claire moved him in a way that was both exciting and disconcerting.

Seeing the back of her head, as she talked to someone and made notes on her computer screen, he slowed down as he approached her cubicle. When another employee tried to acknowledge him, Travis just waved him off, stopping at the back corner of Claire's cubicle and waiting for her to finish her call before announcing himself. His attention was focused on her, and he found the sound of her soft lilting voice, with just a hint of huskiness, very appealing.

Get ahold of yourself, Travis. You're here to convince Claire to help with the new childcare center, not hit on her.

"Miss Workman, was there anything else I can assist you with today?" Claire's voice carried to Travis's ears. She reached up and twirled a long strand of hair while she listened to the voice on the other end of the phone.

"I'm glad. Yes, the same to you. Thank you for shopping with us, and you have a good day." Claire clicked a button on her computer screen. The green light on top turned red, indicating she'd finished the call. She made a few more notes on the computer screen and then pulled her headset off and stretched her arms up above her head.

Travis smiled a bit and then stepped into the doorway of her cubicle where she couldn't help but see him. Her arms froze and then slowly lowered as her expression turned guarded. That fear once more took up residence in her eyes.

"Mr. Hammerstein…"

"Travis," he took a step closer to her, looking at her desk and noting how impersonal it all looked. No family photos or picture frames of any kind sat on the shelf. Stranger yet, not a single Christmas decoration could be seen from where she was sitting. "We need to talk."

Claire shook her head, "I don't believe we do. I'm happy with the position I have right now."

Travis nodded and then met her gaze, "I wasn't actually asking. Please come with me?" He stepped back and gestured toward the elevators. "We don't need an audience for this discussion."

Claire swallowed, and he watched her Adam's apple move, as she went pale again. "Are you firing me?"

Travis frowned and shook his head, "No, nothing of the sort. Please, would you come upstairs with me so that we can talk without all of your co-workers eavesdropping and trying to figure out what they've missed?"

Claire glanced around, spying several of her co-workers, who were stationed close by, duck their heads below the dividers. She nodded. "I'll come with you."

"Good." Travis stepped back and waited, as she idled her computer and then retrieved her purse and jacket. He started to mention that she didn't need those things but then held silent. Only an hour of her workday remained, and this discussion could very well take most of that if things went right. He'd make sure Douglas drove her home, as Steele had confirmed that she used public transportation to and from work. That news hadn't surprised Travis. Parking within the city was completely ridiculous. Very few people actually drove their own personal cars. Instead, they chose to park in designated spots outside the city and ride public transportation to and from their jobs.

Once they reached the elevator, Travis put in his code that took them to the top floor where the executive suite was located. A luxurious apartment was also on this level. Any executives who chose not to travel after a long day at the office were free to use it.

Travis had never used it.

Tyler deserved to have a stable home life and, to that extent, Travis had rented a small house in a gated community about forty-five minutes from the city. He intended to look for a much larger house to buy, but with the Christmas season upon them, he didn't feel like he had time right now to truly devote his attentions to that task. Spring would come soon enough, and he and Tyler would begin looking for a place to call their own.

Part of the commitment Travis had extracted from the Board of Directors was a guarantee that, for the next five years, he could call the shots concerning the running of the department stores, as long as the investors were receiving a positive influx of value. He had also been allowed to choose which store he wanted to make the basis of his operations. He'd naturally chosen Chicago. This was the location of the first store which had been started nearly eighty years earlier by his great-grandparents; a legacy he was proud to continue.

The elevator doors opened, and Travis nodded for Claire to precede him. He led the way toward the opposite end of the space. An executive desk sat in the middle of the walkway, surrounded on both sides by elegant seating areas, nicely cared for potted plants, and sculptures and other works of fine art. Travis's family had either collected them or been given them over the years. He tried to see the space through Claire's eyes and hoped it didn't come off as pretentious, but he thought it might. Travis wasn't like that. While he appreciated fine art, he usually preferred to do so in a museum or art gallery. Since taking control of the company, he'd simply not taken time to change this particular area.

"Sarah, would you please hold all my calls for the rest of the day? In fact, you're welcome to leave a bit early if you like. It was snowing a little bit ago, and the streets are beginning to look a bit slushy."

Sarah was an older woman who had been his grandfather's

administrative assistant and was now his personal secretary. Travis felt very blessed that she'd consented to delay her retirement another year to help him get established in running the corporation. He had until next December to find and train another assistant, but that was something else that could wait until they were well into the New Year.

"Very good, Mr. Hammerstein. Would you care for refreshments for you and your guest before I leave?"

"That would be very nice. Coffee for me. Claire, what would you like to drink?" Travis asked, stopping next to Sarah's desk and looking at her.

"I'm fine," Claire murmured, but he didn't look away. After a long minute, she gave Sarah a tight smile. "Hot tea?"

"Perfect. I'll bring the tray in shortly and then head on home for the evening."

"This way," Travis strode toward his office doors. He opened them wide to allow her to come inside before leaving it slightly ajar for Sarah. "Have a seat over there by the fireplace while I grab a folder from my desk."

He watched Claire slowly walk to the large stone fireplace on the left side of the office space and gingerly sit down in an overstuffed chair. She didn't sit back but sat on the edge with her spine painfully straight. He grabbed his idea folder and then joined her, relaxing back into the opposing chair and crossing one ankle over his knee.

"Relax," he murmured to her. "I promise I don't bite, and this isn't a bad meeting."

Sarah pushed her way into the office, carrying a tray with coffee and tea, and a small plate with Christmas cookies piled artfully on it. She set it on the table between them and then murmured to Travis, "Douglas is on his way up with Tyler. There was a problem at the preschool."

Travis frowned and whispered back, "What kind of problem?"

"Tyler got sick and started crying. They couldn't get him to stop, and he made himself even sicker. They called Douglas to come and get him before he spread his illness to the others."

Travis nodded, realizing this turn of events was going to hamper his efforts with Claire. "Very well. Since he's here, have him drive you home and then come back for us."

"I can take the train…"

"I know you can, but it would please me to know that you were safely delivered home on this snowy evening. I won't have to waste any mental energy wondering over that fact."

Sarah smiled and then nodded, "Very well. Thank you. I'll see you in the morning."

"Unless there's too much snow, then just stay home. It's what I intend to do as well. The forecasters are saying we could get as much as ten inches before morning. I've already instructed Amy in Human Resources to send memos out to all employees asking them to check the company website before leaving for work in the morning. If that much snow falls, the trains and buses will be incapacitated, so we won't even open the store tomorrow. I would rather lose a day's revenue than have our staff and shoppers risking their lives to get here."

"That's exactly what your grandfather would have done," Sarah told him quietly.

Travis felt a sense of pride at her quiet compliment and nodded his head gratefully in acknowledgement. "Thank you. That means a lot coming from you. Good evening."

Sarah smiled warmly at him and then addressed Claire,

"Good evening to you, as well. Please be safe getting home this evening."

"I will," Claire murmured, surprise showing on her face at being included in the conversation.

Sarah left and Travis sighed. "It looks like this meeting may be cut short in a few minutes, but let's get as far as we can. As I told you yesterday, I am making changes here and one of those will be the addition of a childcare center onsite for all employees to utilize. You happen to have the right qualifications to help us achieve this. I would be very appreciative if you would reconsider your answer."

Claire looked at him and then shook her head. "I can't."

Travis steepled his fingers and chuckled. "Unfortunately for you, that word has never been part of my vocabulary. So, tell me why you can't, and I will help you find that you can."

Claire looked at him and then away, worrying her fingers to the point that he wondered if she wasn't in pain. When she continued to look away, and then he saw a tear roll down her cheek, Travis wanted nothing more than to pull her into his arms, which was a strange reaction given he'd just met her.

"Claire, talk to me. I know we've just met, and you don't know me at all, but I'm here to help. Really."

She shook her head and murmured, wiping her cheek, but still refusing to look at him. "Thank you for the offer, but there isn't anything anyone can do." She took a calming breath and then glanced at him before directing her eyes just over his shoulder. "I appreciate you giving me the opportunity but, believe me, I am the last person you should be considering for this position."

"You're a licensed daycare provider with all of the right certifications. I've done my homework. Your licensing is still valid for another three years."

45

"I haven't worked with children for a very long time. I wouldn't be a good fit," she countered back.

"Why not? I should tell you that I contacted the previous preschool you ran and was surprised to find out that you had owned it at one time. The director there was very complimentary about you and asked me to convey her happiness that you were getting back to your true calling."

"You talked with Shelly?" Claire asked, her face going pale white.

"Yes, I believe that was her name. She asked about you as well, and I encouraged her to give you a call."

"You shouldn't have done that," Claire told him, shaking her head.

"Why not? Do you not want to talk to her? She sounded as if you two had been friends."

"At one time, but I haven't talked to her in four years."

"That's a rather long time. That would have been about the time you sold her your preschool."

Claire nodded.

"So, tell me why a young woman who, according to Shelly, has a calling to work with young children, is answering phones in my call center?"

"Knock, knock," Douglas called from the doorway, striding in with Tyler in his arms. "Sorry to interrupt. Did Sarah tell you I called?"

"She did," Travis got up and met Douglas in the center of the room. "I'll take him. I told Sarah you would drive her home."

"I'd already offered as well. It's getting pretty bad out there. I'll run her out and then come back for you and the little man here."

Travis took Tyler into his arms, frowning at the sour smell coming from his shirt. Douglas saw it and nodded, "He threw up again in the car. Luckily, I just unbuckled him and most of it went on the pavement. You're smelling what hit him."

Travis nodded and then asked, "How did you manage not to get baptized?"

"Quick reflexes and six nieces and nephews. I'll be back shortly. Feel better, Ty."

Travis turned as Douglas left, and then froze when he saw Claire watching them with her hand over her mouth and tears streaming down her face. He hugged Tyler closer to him and then walked toward her, slowing down when she stood up and tried to back away from them. "Claire?"

"I...I can't do this...I'm sorry..." She reached for her purse and coat and tried to scoot around the chair to escape his office, but Travis wasn't letting her runaway this time.

"Stop!" He reached the small couch and laid Tyler down, patting his shoulder when his son immediately rolled over and closed his eyes. "Whatever is wrong, running away isn't going to fix it." Travis kept his voice low, both for his son and her benefit.

"You don't understand," she told him in a low tearful voice. "There is no 'fix' for this problem."

"That's where you're wrong. Tell me that running away yesterday made you feel better. If you can, I'll escort you to the elevator myself," he challenged her.

***

Hope was watching the interaction between Travis and Claire with interest. When Travis challenged her, she knew Claire couldn't tell him that. She'd been miserable all night long, plagued with memories of the past and the bleakness of her future.

47

Hope had been following Claire closely all day, hoping to find some way of helping her begin to deal with the past. When Travis had shown up and insisted that she join him in his office, Hope had finally found something that she might be able to use. It seemed that Travis was attracted to Claire. Though Claire was trying to ignore her body, she found Travis just as attractive. It was a start. Hope was going to give them every little bit of help she could that was within the guidelines of the rules and regulations which the guardian angels had to follow.

Tyler started to stir, so Hope hovered over the couch and sent calming thoughts to the little boy. He needed to continue to rest his sick body and let his father try to help Claire lance the wound that had been festering for far too long.

This moment, right here, could very well be the turning point for both of her charges. She watched, asking for a little heavenly grace and blessing for both of them, as she waited to see if Claire would exhibit strength which Matthias was convinced she had. This moment could very well be the beginning of healing for the young woman who had suffered losses no person should have to endure, but many did. She just needed to take a step of faith and open herself up to Travis. Then, maybe together, they could both begin to heal from the past and find a better and happier future for themselves.

Chapter 5

Claire was barely holding herself together. Try as she might, she couldn't answer Travis's question truthfully and gain her freedom from this conversation. She'd fallen apart yesterday. Running off to be alone had only made the memories and emotions more vivid. There'd been no one to share her grief with, not that she'd ever taken a trip down that particular path.

When she'd seen the other man walk into the office with the little boy held in his arms, she hadn't seen Travis's son but her own. She hadn't been holding Daniel when he'd died. His injuries had been so severe, his little hand had been all she could safely clasp, but it hadn't been enough. She hadn't been able to hold him close or tell him how much she'd loved him. He'd died all alone in that hospital bed.

Her tears had started flowing down her cheeks unchecked. When Travis had drawn closer with Tyler in his arms, she'd just needed to put some distance between them. It was obvious the little boy was sick. His face was pale, and his skin appeared clammy. The stains on the front of his shirt told the rest of the story. Travis no longer was holding his son, having put him down to try to deal with her...just another thing for her to feel guilty about.

He should be caring for his son, not trying to handle my problems. I need to get out of here.

Claire looked at him, and then his son let out a small whimper and drew her focus. He turned toward them. She could see from several feet away that his face was flushed, and his hair was soaked with sweat. The poor baby was running a fever. Given the way he was squirming, she guessed he also had a tummy ache.

The phone on Travis's desk rang and he shot it a look of disgust. "I thought I told Sarah to hold all of my calls."

"You already sent her home," Claire reminded him quietly.

Travis sent her a look and then his shoulders sagged, "So I did. I need to get this. Promise me you won't leave until we finish our discussion?"

Claire nodded wearily, somehow knowing that if she ran again, he would just find another opportunity to try and have this discussion. He would eventually wear her down, so she might as well stay and rip the bandage all the way off now. She could then go home and wallow in self-pity and guilt for the remainder of the night. The phone rang again, and she waved him toward his desk.

"I'll wait."

To emphasize her commitment, she sat back down in the chair and crossed her arms over her chest. Travis nodded his approval and then strode across the carpet on silent feet. He picked up the phone on the third ring.

"Yes?"

Claire listened to him, but her gaze was focused on the little boy who had settled back down again on the couch. He looked so much like Daniel had at that age. His hair had been straight yesterday but, now that it was wet, it had curled up on his forehead. She guessed he must be close to four-years old, given his size. She was watching him when his eyes suddenly opened, and he was watching her back.

She unconsciously held her breath, as she waited to see what he would do. He lay there, obviously uncomfortable but seeming content to just watch her. Travis was talking on the phone about some breach in security down on the retail floor. He sounded irritated, and she lifted her head, surprised to see him shove a hand through his hair in frustration.

She frowned for a minute as she watched him, which is why she was so surprised when a small body pressed itself against her knees a moment later. She jerked and looked down to see the little boy standing next to her chair, leaning heavily on her as he reached for her, wanting to be picked up. Claire felt her heart seize, and she swallowed back a cry of despair.

"Are you sad?" his little voice asked.

She looked into his feverish eyes, and the compassion she'd buried deep surged to the surface. She was reaching for him before she could stop herself. When he wrapped his arms around her neck and buried his damp forehead against her shoulder, she could only sit there holding him while tears streamed down her cheeks.

"Don't cry lady." The little boy reached up a small hand and patted her cheek.

Claire closed her eyes, absorbing the feel of the little body in her arms. She grieved for all the days and months she hadn't had this particular pleasure.

"Shush. Just rest, baby."

"I got sick all over."

"I know, but you'll feel better soon."

She cradled him close, relieved when he stopped talking and laid his head upon her shoulder once more. She felt his body relax and knew the minute he fell back to sleep, but it didn't lessen her grief any. She leaned her head back and prayed to a God she'd all but forsaken four years ago for the strength to make it through the next few minutes. Her soul was raw. Her pain was so intense that she physically hurt.

Somewhere in the back of her consciousness, she heard Travis end the call. Then, he was there, squatting down next to her chair with tissues in hand. "I can take him."

Claire opened her eyes and nodded, but she couldn't make her arms let go. "I'm... I'm sorry."

"Shush. Do you want me to take him?" Travis asked in a whisper.

Claire swallowed hard and then shook her head once, "No. He's sleeping."

She sniffed, trying to regain control of her emotions. It took several tries before she was able to stop her tears. She reached for the tissues, but Travis evaded her hand and gently wiped them away himself. The moment was so intimate, Claire stared into Travis's eyes and held her breath. Her body responded to his kindness and the compassion she sensed. She longed to throw herself into his arms and beg him to make the hurt go away, which confused her something fierce. She didn't really know this man, so why did she have the sudden urge to unburden her soul to him? It didn't make any sense at all and was a recipe for disaster and heartbreak.

After several minutes, the little boy stirred once more. He opened his eyes and immediately reached for his father. Travis took him and, after getting him resettled on the couch, he turned and motioned for Claire to join him.

She stood up, unable to find any strength left to fight him or herself. She went to him, surprised when he took her hand and pulled her over to the wall of windows that offered a view of Lake Michigan. He stood beside her, holding her hand in a comforting gesture, but said nothing.

Claire relaxed minute by minute, as she realized he was offering her his support without demanding anything in return. After fifteen minutes, she turned to look at him and blushed when she realized he had been staring at her.

"Thank you."

Travis nodded and then asked, "Want to talk now?"

Claire rolled her eyes, "No, but I've been saying that for the last four years."

Travis gave her a sympathetic look and then turned toward her, "I have a suggestion, if you'll hear me out?" When she nodded, he continued, "I need to get Tyler home…"

"Tyler," she murmured almost to herself. When Travis raised a brow, she explained, "I wasn't sure of his name."

"Now you know. Anyway, as you can probably tell, he's not feeling very well, and I need to get him home as soon as Douglas gets back. The roads are getting pretty slushy out there as well, so what I am proposing is that we move this meeting to my temporary home, order some dinner, and then Douglas will drive you home a bit later."

Claire immediately started shaking her head, "I don't think that's a good idea."

"Please? I have to admit; this is the first time Tyler's been sick like this, and I'm a little out of my league here."

"I'm sure your wife will know what to do," she murmured, automatically looking over to check on the small boy.

"I'm going to assume by that statement that the corporate gossip mill hasn't made it to your desk yet." When she raised a questioning brow, he explained, "My wife passed away when Tyler was eighteen months old."

Claire felt a wave of sorrow move through her for his loss. She knew exactly how losing someone you were supposed to grow old with felt. It was soul wrenching. She shook her head. "I'm sorry. I shouldn't have said…well, anyway. I'm sorry for your loss. And his."

"We're coping the best we can. Honestly, Tyler doesn't even remember Emily. As for me, some days I find it hard to think about her. We thought we had the perfect life; I never dreamed it would be taken away so quickly or in such a devastating way. By the time they discovered that she had a rare form of cancer, it had spread to every major organ in her body. Her last few weeks were filled with her being drugged with Morphine to dull the pain that wracked her body. She went fast but watching her go through that...it makes remembering what she was like before really hard sometimes."

Claire's heart went out to him. For all of her own suffering, she hadn't had to watch Scott or Daniel die over the course of weeks. Her torment had been short-lived. Nonetheless, it had been devastating. She couldn't imagine having had to watch Daniel suffer for weeks instead of days.

A knock on the door announced the return of Douglas, and the need for Claire to make a decision. Part of her wanted to run away to her lonely apartment where she could give way to the emotions of the day. The other part of her, the part that had felt joy in holding Tyler in her arms, urged her to go with Travis and finally share her past with someone. And not just anyone, but someone who would fully understand where she was at emotionally and psychologically, because he'd been there himself. He'd lost someone close to him, and he was moving on with his life.

Maybe I could learn a thing or two from him. I can't keep going this way, that much is obvious. I've been hiding from the pain for much too long.

"Claire?" Travis asked, waiting for her answer.

She nodded, unable to find her voice as she just agreed to bare her soul.

"Good. Let me get Tyler bundled up, then we'll head out. Claire, meet Douglas. Douglas, Claire is going to join Tyler and I for some dinner while we finish our discussion and then I promised you would see her home later."

"I'd be happy to. The roads are getting rather nasty and they just announced the trains will stop at midnight, if not sooner. They've already cancelled schools and all government offices tomorrow and are encouraging other businesses to follow suit."

Travis nodded as he grabbed Tyler's coat and headed for the couch. "Let me get Tyler taken care of and then I'll need to place a call and make sure the word gets out to all of our employees."

Ten minutes later, Claire accompanied the other three males down to the parking garage. As they pulled out onto the street, she was shocked to see how much snow had already fallen on the city. The traffic was already thinning out as everyone headed to their respective homes for the evening. "I don't think I've ever seen this much snow here."

"The radio announcer said this is supposed to be a record-setting storm. They are expecting another ten inches before morning." Douglas met Travis's eyes through the rearview mirror.

Another ten inches of snow?

Claire was stunned, as she tried to imagine what that would look like outside on the city streets.

"I thought they were only expecting ten inches total?" Travis asked.

"They've now changed that to around sixteen inches."

"That's a lot of snow," Claire murmured, wondering how a city the size of Chicago could possibly deal with that much snow. "Where do they put it?"

"In the lake, if it's close enough. Otherwise, they'll load it into dump trucks and haul it outside the city and dump it there."

Claire opened her mouth to ask another question, but she was stopped when Tyler woke up, saw her, and immediately climbed into her lap and snuggled up against her chest. Her arms, once again, automatically closed around him, and thankfully the waterworks didn't start up again. She looked up and could tell Travis was waiting for her tears, so she gave him a tremulous smile.

"He's burning up with fever," she whispered.

"I have some medicine for that at home," he whispered back.

"As long as it isn't Aspirin," she cautioned him.

"Why no Aspirin?"

"Young children can get something called Reye Syndrome from taking Aspirin to break a fever when they have a viral infection."

"I've never heard of that," Travis told her.

"It's pretty rare these days, and all Aspirin bottles have a warning label on them. The illness affects the brain and liver function and children have died from it."

"Is this the preschool director talking?" Travis asked her.

Claire shrugged, "Probably. You'd be surprised how many first-time parents would freak out when their child got sick for the first time. It's inevitable when they are around other kids a lot, but it can also be really scary."

"I didn't say I was scared," Travis told her.

"No, you didn't. I was talking in general terms." She well remembered the first time Daniel had gotten sick and ran a high fever. All of her consoling words disappeared, and she'd made Scott drive them to the emergency room, where the nurses and doctors there had gently explained Daniel had a viral infection and there was nothing to do but treat the symptoms and allow his body time to fight off the infection.

"Well, I admit to being a bit less confident than I like, and I thank you for agreeing to move this meeting to my home. I'll also take any advice you want to offer."

Claire nodded her head and then turned her attention out the window. She watched the landscape pass them by, her arms full of little boy, and the ice around her heart starting to sweat.

God - don't let me fall apart like I did four years ago. I know I haven't talked to you in a long while...I'd apologize, but I'm still not sure how to process losing Scott and Daniel. You could have saved them, and I don't understand why you didn't. I feel like you let me down. I don't know why Travis and Tyler have come into my life right now. I know You're supposed to be working everything out for my good, but taking my husband and son, and then my precious innocent baby away...how could that ever be considered good? I just don't understand...

"You okay over there?" Travis whispered.

Claire shook her head, "Not even close. Do you believe in God?"

Travis took a deep breath and then let it out, "Yes, but He and I aren't on the best of terms right now. You?"

"I do, but I'm kind of in the same position. He let me down, and I'm still really mad about that. Guess that makes me a rotten person, huh?"

Travis was silent for a moment and then shook his head, "No, I think it just makes you human. I like to think that God welcomes all of our emotions, even the ones we think are ugly and wrong. If they are honest."

Travis was quiet for a long moment and then added, "When Emily first was diagnosed, I was furious with God. I demanded answers, practically begging him to heal her. She had a little boy to raise...at one point I even offered to change places with her. I would have gladly gone through the chemo and radiation treatments if it would have meant she didn't have to."

"God wasn't listening," Claire murmured.

Travis touched her cheek, waiting to speak until she was

looking directly at him. "God heard every word I said, but for some reason, Emily's time on this earth was over."

"Some reason?" Claire questioned, derisively. "What reason could possibly justify your son losing his mother, and you losing your wife?"

"That's the hard part, isn't it?" Travis agreed. "Believe me, I railed at God and demanded answers, but I never got them. My mom reminded me that God's ways are not our own and that I may never know why my wife had to suffer. I simply have to live by faith and with the knowledge that there is a higher plan and purpose at work here."

Claire thought about that as the car continued departing the city. She'd always thought it was wrong to question God or be upset with Him for the way things turned out. She'd never really given herself permission to actually be mad at Him, even though that's exactly how she felt. She was mad at God. Furious even.

Is that honest enough for You? I guess if Travis is right, then You must have the answers for how I get from where I am to where I used to be. I hate living like this. I hate it.

***

Hope was both happy, and sad, for the way her two charges were handling their problems. She was elated that they seemed to be pulling closer to one another and possibly working on handling their problems as a team, but she didn't like the idea that Claire was mad at God. That presented another aspect of Claire's situation Hope hadn't planned on.

She watched as they arrived at Travis's temporary living space, and she hovered nearby while Claire helped him figure out the dosage of the over the counter, non-Aspirin-based fever reducer to give him. It seemed that once Claire had gotten past the initial shock of holding a small boy in her arms again, her emotions seemed to be settling down. Her maternal instincts kicked in, and she couldn't fight the desire to help make Tyler feel better.

I wonder if interacting with him is also making her feel better? I wonder if she will even recognize that?

After getting Tyler settled into his pajamas and safely asleep on the couch in the large room that eventually flowed into the dining room and kitchen, Travis suggested they see about dinner. With the weather outside, ordering something to be delivered was out, so Travis suggested they make a simple meal of omelets.

"You cook?" Claire asked, a note of disbelief in her voice.

"Doesn't every man?" Travis countered back, as he started pulling things from the refrigerator. Claire seated herself on a barstool to watch.

Claire gave a derisive laugh and shook her head, "Not any man I've ever met that wasn't getting paid to do so. My husband could burn water…"

She broke her sentence when she realized what she'd just said. Hope moved closer, spreading her wings and trying to offer a sense of security to the gaping chasm that Claire's words had just opened up. Claire didn't speak about her late husband and, to Travis's credit, he didn't act surprised or demand more answers.

He simply watched her from time to time, as he started cracking eggs into a bowl and then began whisking them together. Several minutes went by before Claire finally spoke up again.

Be strong, Claire. You can do this. Say the words and release some of the pain.

Hope was doing what she could to encourage the young woman to take a leap of faith. She was almost ready to give up, when something inside Claire seemed to burst wide open.

"It's been almost four years since I've said those words," she offered quietly into the void

"You don't like to talk about your husband?"

Claire shook her head, "It's not a matter of liking. I just don't. I haven't...I mean...well, I haven't up until now. Does that make me a horrible person? That I've tried to shut thoughts of him completely away?"

Travis expertly flipped the first omelet and then met her eyes. "I think it makes you human and shows that you were just trying to survive. Can I ask what happened to him?"

Hope watched as Claire's face drained of all color. Would she take the opening she'd just been given to start the healing process, or would she stay locked away in her self-imposed lonely prison of pain? Hope held her breath, as she waited to see what Claire would do.

Chapter 6

"He died." Claire uttered the words through stiff lips, afraid that speaking them out loud would bring her world crashing down around her shoulders. She kept her eyes on the marble countertop, waiting for Travis to press for more of an answer, but he surprised her again.

"I'm sorry. I know what that feels like."

When he didn't say anything else, she looked up and watched as he slid the omelets out of the pan and onto two plates. He slid one to her and then opened up the refrigerator again, "What would you like to drink? Soda. Water. Juice. I don't drink so…"

"I don't either," she murmured. "Water is fine."

Travis pulled two bottles of water from the door of the refrigerator and then handed one to her before walking around and seating himself on the adjacent barstool. He nodded at her plate, "Eat up before it gets cold, and then I'd like to go over my childcare center idea with you."

Claire was speechless. After he started eating, she did the same. He was giving her as much room as she needed and letting her tell him what she wanted about her past, without any pressure to fill in the details or explain why she'd never dealt with her grief before now. It was refreshing, and a huge relief to know that he was supporting her just by being present.

She started eating, amazed at how he'd constructed something so simple and yet with so much flavor. "Travis, this is really good."

"Thanks. I can't cook a lot of things, but I can do eggs about twelve different ways."

"Twelve?" she asked with lilt in her voice. "I didn't know there were twelve ways to do eggs."

He looked at her and Hope could feel Claire's emotions start to unwind as her color returned. "That would be where you just haven't taken the time to count them."

Claire smiled, and Hope felt like doing a little dance. The young woman had opened the door to her past and had lived to enjoy the present. She didn't wait around to see how the rest of the evening was going to go. She headed back up to the heavenly realm, needing to share what she considered a victory with someone. Anyone. Maybe Claire wasn't as broken as she thought she was. Hope just needed to continue to show her how beautiful life and the Christmas season was.

"I'll name them, oh ye of little faith. Scrambled, of course. Fried. Poached. Hard-boiled. Soft-boiled."

"Aren't those kind of the same thing?" she asked dubiously.

"Not at all. A perfectly cooked soft-boiled egg has the whites cooked till firm, but the yolk is still nice and gooey."

Claire choked on a drink of her water, "Gooey eggs?"

"My term. Anyway, let's see that was five. Deviled. Pickled."

"Ew. No thanks."

"Me either," Travis agreed. "That's one version I will never personally make."

"Good. Okay, so that's seven. You still need five more."

"Okay, so there are omelets, quiches, eggs benedict – my personal favorite, egg salad, and shirred eggs."

"Shirred eggs? What are those?"

"Basically, it's a baked egg where the yolk isn't broken."

"Oh, I haven't ever tried to cook an egg that way."

"I've only done it once and decided it took too much time. Eggs are supposed to be a quick meal."

"I agree."

"So, do you cook?" Travis asked.

"Not as much as I used to," she told him softly, trying not to let the memories swarm in like bees. "It's just me. Most nights, I'm so tired by the time I get home, I just heat up some soup or make a sandwich and go to bed while watching television."

"That actually sounds pretty depressing."

Claire agreed but remained silent on the matter. They both finished eating and she insisted on helping clean up since he'd done the cooking. Once the kitchen was restored to its previous organized splendor, Travis checked on Tyler and then retrieved a folder he'd brought from the office.

"Here are my projections and ideas for the childcare center. The Chicago store will be a test run, and we'll need to make changes and adjustments as we go before implementing it anywhere else."

Claire's palms were sweating, as she reached for the folder. Travis had been nothing but kind and the slight attraction she'd felt for him earlier was even more pronounced now. "I'll look at them, but I'm still not ready to take the position."

"Look my ideas over and, for now, just agree to help me get everything in order so that we can apply for the permit and proper licenses."

"I can do that," Claire agreed. She opened the folder, amazed at how thoroughly Travis had researched this new project. He had estimates on the cost to retrofit the fourth floor of the building. An indoor play area, plus learning zones, a small kitchen, even an area where children could nap without being disturbed by others that were wide awake."

She found the permits already filled out and immediately saw a few errors. "This number is wrong," she pointed to the student to teacher ratio for children younger than twelve months. "The state requires a smaller number of children to each teacher or teacher's assistant when dealing with infants."

Travis handed her a pen, "Feel free to make any changes you need to. I prefer to do things right the first time, so that I don't have to do them again."

"Me too," Claire agreed. She made a few adjustments as she read through the remaining pages and then looked up, "These look good, you just need to fix a few numbers here and there."

"Do you think the state will fight us on this? I heard they sometimes have a problem with daycare centers not being on the ground floor."

"That's going to be a hurdle you'll have to fix. The building codes have been in place a long time and they won't change them. It's just not safe. Little kids can't very well get themselves out of a building if it catches on fire. They also wouldn't be able to use the elevator or descend flights of stairs on their own."

"How do hospitals manage to have nurseries not on the ground floor?"

"I don't know, but I'm sure it has to do with the fire suppression system and the general emergency response plan. I personally never liked having the children I was supervising on anything other than the ground floor. I know some people argue it makes them more vulnerable to anyone coming in off the street who might want to create terror, but I'd rather risk that than have to figure out how to get thirty two and three-year olds down four flights of stairs in the event of an emergency."

"I guess I hadn't really thought that part through," Travis told her.

"What floor were you planning on using?"

"The fourth?"

Claire shook her head, "You'll never get approval for that. It would be better to move part of the warehouse to the fourth floor and revamp that street-level space."

"I see you've thought about this."

"Not really, I'm just being realistic. You can't very well redesign the store itself. The warehouse space is the only movable department in the right space."

Travis nodded and then pulled out his phone and sent off a text message. "Done."

"What?"

"The warehouse will begin moving to the fourth floor just as soon as this storm passes."

"Why would you do that?"

"What? Take your advice? Of course, I'm going to take your advice. I don't do half measures. I want this to be the best childcare center in the city."

"What about security?" she asked, thinking about the large bay doors all along the backside of the building.

"I'll have a crew come in and wall off the receiving area. There are large service elevators at either end, so they can use those to move the freight upstairs. The rest of the space will be under constant surveillance and parents will have to check their children in and out."

Claire closed the folder and slid it back to him. "Well, you've just taken care of the major objection I saw. Your idea for the design is amazing."

Travis smiled, "So, have I tempted you to supervise it yet?"

Claire shook her head. "I'm really not the right person for this project."

"I think you are. Whatever tragedies you haven't told me yet, you've proven to me and hopefully to yourself, that you are strong enough to handle them."

"That's where you're wrong. I'm not strong at all. Most people deal with their grief. They cry and carry on, even go into a depression for a while, but then they pick themselves up and get back to living. They don't bury everything, so they don't have to deal with it. They don't act the coward."

"You are not a coward," Travis told her.

"You can say that, but you don't know…I ran away. Yesterday. The day before. Four years ago. That's what I do, I run. It's supposed to be safer that way."

"And much lonelier and harder to get over the past."

"Who helped you?" she asked.

"Family. Friends."

"Be thankful you had those things. I had no one."

"Not a single person?"

"The two police officers who brought the news stayed with

me, but I barely knew them from high school. They felt sorry for me, and I felt like a charity case." That wasn't quite accurate, but it helped Claire feel justified in how she'd dealt with the past.

"I'm sure they didn't mean for you to feel that way."

Claire shrugged, "It doesn't matter now. I was alone, and I did what I needed to survive."

"That was then. How about you stop running and hiding and face the past? I promise you won't have to do it alone."

"You're going to hold my hand while I fall apart?" she asked incredulously.

"Yes."

"Why?"

Travis smiled at her, "Because I like you, and you're hurting. I hate the idea that you had to go through whatever trauma occurred all by yourself. Give me a chance to be the shoulder you needed four years ago."

"I still don't understand why you would want to do that? What's in it for you?"

"A chance to help a fellow human being who just happens to be gorgeous and someone I really hope is going to give me a chance to get to know her better. There's something about you that calls to me."

Claire stared at him, "So, you're offering to be what, my friend?"

"To begin with."

To begin with? Does he think we might become romantically involved? I mean, he's one of the most handsome men I've met, and we have a lot in common, but I don't think that I ever want to risk my heart again. Maybe I don't even have a heart left that could fall in love.

"Tell you what, why don't you take the folder home with you and think about it. The store is closed tomorrow and possibly the day after. We'll get together two days from now and we can discuss your involvement in the project at that time."

Claire nodded, "Okay. I don't work over the weekend."

"We'll meet on Monday. I'll have Sarah call down to your desk when I have an opening."

"Fine," Claire nodded and then walked over to retrieve her coat and purse. Tyler was still sound asleep on the couch, and she couldn't resist going over and feeling his forehead. "The fever's broken."

Travis joined her. "Good. Will he need more medicine?"

"Just keep an eye on him and check him in a few hours. What you gave him should last four to six hours."

"Okay. I'm glad you were here to help me," Travis told her, taking her coat and holding it out for her to slip her arms in.

She did so and, when Travis slid his hands beneath the fall of her hair to pull it out of the collar, she bit her lip. The feel of his hands on the back of her neck robbed her of breath. Was there a possibility of having more than friendship between them? She stepped away from him and forced a smile.

"Thank you for dinner."

"My pleasure. Douglas is waiting in the garage with the car." Travis walked her to the doorway and then to the car. When he started to open the back door, she shook her head and stood before the front passenger door.

"I'd rather ride up here, if that's okay."

"That's fine with me, miss."

"Very well," Travis opened the door and then waited until she'd fastened her seatbelt to say, "Be safe and feel free to jot down any notes or suggestions you might have. We'll discuss them in a few days. Douglas, Claire will give you her address."

"Very good. Would you like me to stop and get anything for Tyler before I come back?"

"I think we're okay. Be careful out there."

"I'll send you a text message when I get back. If you need me during the night, you know how to get ahold of me."

"Sounds good. Claire, thank you again. Goodnight."

"Goodnight," she murmured, as he shut the door, and Douglas opened up the garage door. Tonight had been full of surprises. She tried to compartmentalize everything that had transpired since Travis had shown up at her cubicle, but her brain was too tired. She decided she needed a good night's sleep before she tackled the problem of Travis and his childcare center. There would be plenty of time for that later.

Chapter 7

Two days later…

Claire was making herself crazy. After leaving Travis's, she'd gone directly to bed. The folder he'd insisted she take waited for her attention on the kitchen table. She'd managed to ignore it for an entire twenty-four hours before she'd finally given in and taken a closer look at his plans.

She had to admit; they were very well thought out. The benefit to the Hammerstein employees would go way beyond just a financial one. They would be able to bring their children to work with them, eliminating the need for extra trips to daycare centers around the city. They wouldn't have to worry about picking them up on time, as they would merely be an elevator's ride away. The costs Travis was suggesting were ridiculously low, but if employee attendance improved, the costs would be made up in the long run.

She spent almost three hours going over every piece of paper, checking to make sure he'd met all of the state requirements, and making notations on things that absolutely had to be changed, and other things that would benefit from some tweaking and the reasons why. When she finally put the folder down, she was exhausted once again. She heated up a cup of soup and crawled back into bed.

She'd been struggling with the idea that Travis wanted her to take over this project and run the Chicago center. In order to do that, she would have to confront the past in more ways than one. She would need to gain access to her license from the state, but she didn't have it. She'd left everything at the preschool, and it was very possible that it had been thrown out along with the other items in her house that she'd abandoned.

She picked up the picture on her bedside table. It was the only one she had of Scott and Daniel. A wave of sorrow brought tears to her eyes. In her attempt to run away from the emotions brought on by their deaths, she'd also given up everything that she'd once held dear. Before their deaths, she had set aside everything to remember the good times when everyone was older. She'd left it all behind and now she was filled with regret.

She eyed the clock on the dresser and then picked up her cell phone to stare at the numbers for several minutes. Was she brave enough to place a simple phone call?

Shelly.

She sat up in the bed, pushed herself up against the headboard, and dialed the number she'd known by heart for almost a decade. She hesitated only a moment before hitting the green phone icon and then pulled her hand away quickly, so that she wouldn't stop the call from connecting. She pressed the speaker button, and then placed the phone on her lap. When it started to ring, she eyed it like it was a viper getting ready to strike.

"Hello?"

Claire felt her breath stall at the sound of the familiar voice. She opened her mouth to respond, but nothing came out but a puff of air.

"Hello? Is anyone there?" Another pause and then Shelly gave an exasperated sigh, "Look, you called me. Either identify yourself, or I'm going to hang up and block this number. Last chance. Three. Two."

"Shelly?" Claire's voice sounded scratchy, so she tried again, "Shelly, please don't hang up. It's me. Claire."

There was a long pause and then Shelly asked, "Claire? Claire, is that really you?"

"Yes."

"Oh, my Lord. Where are you? Are you okay?"

"I'm fine." Understatement of the year, but Claire was trying to maintain control of her emotions. She didn't dare give voice to how she was truly feeling.

"Oh, goodness, now I'm crying. Just a minute. Don't hang up."

Claire smiled, remembering that Shelly was one to cry at the littlest thing. A *Hallmark Movie*, a picture drawn by a three-year old, a video of cute puppies…they were all guaranteed to make her tear up.

"I'm back. Oh, Claire. It's so good to hear your voice. I've missed you…we've all missed you so much."

We?

"Thanks," Claire told her, uncomfortable with the knowledge that Shelly had missed and worried about her. "Um, I was calling to ask…I know I don't have the right to, but would my license paperwork happen to be around still?"

"Of course, it is. I put it and a bunch of your other paperwork in a box for safekeeping, hoping one day you would come back for them."

She kept my things?

Claire felt a sense of relief, but also dread, knowing that she would need to make a trip back there to retrieve her things. That would mean seeing people she'd known before the funeral. She looked at the picture of Scott and Daniel and wasn't sure she had the strength to do this. She'd be all alone and, if she fell apart again…

"I…thank you."

"Are you coming back home?" Shelly asked. "I would love to have some more help at the preschool…"

"I don't live there any longer. I moved to Chicago."

"Chicago? What are you doing in the big city? You always said you hated how impersonal the people were there."

"People change," Claire murmured. "Anyway, I guess I need to make arrangements to come and get my license and whatever else you stored for me."

"Anytime. Just tell me when you're going to make the drive, and I'll make sure I've got the time free," Shelly told her.

Claire bit her bottom lip. If she put this off, she would find a million reasons to never go. She had a few days of personal time coming, and she could take Monday off from work with a simple email to Steele. He'd be nosy when she returned and want details she'd rather not give out, but that was a price she was willing to pay. Suddenly, having any sort of memorabilia in her possession seemed like the most important thing in the world.

"I'll be coming up Monday morning and be there between noon and one o'clock? Does that work?"

"That will be perfect. Monday is one of our lighter days. Oh, I'm so excited," Shelly laughed into the phone. "You'll come to the preschool?"

"Yes," Claire told her, digging her fingernails into her free palm, as she resisted trying to arrange a different meeting place. "I'm looking forward to it as well."

Liar, liar, pants on fire. The last place you want to be is back where you won't be able to get away from the memories.

"Great. I'm so glad you called. I'm going to save your number and then we just have to stay in touch," Shelly told her.

"Sure," Claire agreed. "Hey, there's someone at my door. I'll see you Monday."

"You sure will. Drive safe."

Claire disconnected the call and then stared at her phone. "What have I done?" Her hands were shaking as she picked up the picture. She so badly needed a distraction from what she'd just agreed to do. Anything to keep her from calling Shelly back and telling her it had all been a mistake and she wasn't coming to see her.

She crawled from the bed and paced to the living room but moving didn't help. She headed for the kitchen, thinking she'd take a page from her late mother's book and bake something. Anything, even if it wasn't edible. It would keep her occupied and hopefully she wouldn't give into the panic that was threatening to take over.

She grabbed a large mixing bowl, the container of flour and was reaching for a cookbook when the bell chimed, indicating someone was down in the foyer wanting to come up. It was only seven o'clock, but she never had visitors and decided to ignore it.

Someone pushed the wrong apartment number.

She flipped the cookbook open, but the bell chimed again. Puzzled, she walked over to the intercom and pressed the button, "Yes?"

"Claire? It's Travis. Can I come up and talk to you for a minute?"

Travis is downstairs in the foyer? What is he doing here?

"Um…sure…I guess…"

"Great. Buzz me up."

Claire did so and then looked down at what she was wearing.

Pajama pants and a t-shirt, minus a bra because she hadn't been expecting to see anyone. She dashed for the bedroom, grabbed a bra and quickly put it on, and was just pulling on a clean t-shirt when Travis knocked on her apartment door.

"Coming," she called out. She walked to the door, thankful that she was what some would call a neat freak. No dirty socks would be found lying under the couch and she abhorred fast food so empty pizza boxes were also missing from her décor.

She removed the locks and then opened the door, surprised to see Travis standing there with snow melting in his hair. "You've been outside."

"Yeah, I had Douglas drop me off at the street and then I ended up holding the door for the older woman who lives downstairs."

"She's the superintendent of the building," Claire offered, stepping back and allowing him to come inside. She headed to the kitchen and retrieved a clean towel, surprised that he was standing so close when she turned to hand it to him.

"Thanks," Travis smiled and took the towel. Claire backed up a step.

"What are you doing here? Is Tyler okay?"

"Tyler's doing great. He's actually sound asleep in the car, or I would have brought him up with me. He just had a twenty-four bug and is back to his usual exuberant self today."

"I'm glad. Most childhood illnesses don't last very long."

"That's good to know. Anyway, I was on this side of town and thought I'd check to see if you had time to go over the childcare info?"

"I did," Claire murmured. *And it made me do something I'm*

probably going to regret.

"And?" Travis asked, moving out of her kitchen and wandering around her living room. "This room is really peaceful."

Claire nodded and then joined him, "I made a few notes, but most of your ideas look sound." She picked up the folder and handed it to him.

"Sound. Well, I don't know if that was the word I was looking for," he told her, opening up the folder and glancing at her suggestions for several minutes. He nodded and made small noises, and Claire finally sat down, pulling her legs up onto the seat with her.

"You made some good points in here. Thank you. So, you were also supposed to be thinking about my offer."

Claire looked down and suddenly a rash idea came into her mind and she blurted out, "I need you to come to Winchester, Illinois with me Monday."

Travis raised a brow, "I asked you to be the director of a childcare center and instead you want me to go to some little town in Illinois?" When she didn't say anything, he opened his mouth and then nodded, "Wait. Winchester is where your preschool was located, wasn't it?"

"Yes. I need to be there around noon or a little after." Claire finally met his eyes and hoped that he couldn't see how desperately she needed him to agree, but on the other hand, was hoping he would refuse so that she had an excuse not to go herself.

"What's in Winchester?" Travis asked, sitting down on the couch next to her chair.

"My license."

"Does that mean what I think it means?"

"I'm willing to try the new position, but if it's too much, I will agree to help interview and train another person who can do the job."

"A year," Travis told her.

"A year for what?"

"A year. That's how much time I want you to commit to the position before you throw in the towel. Twelve months."

Claire shook her head, "No way. I'll know within a few weeks if this is going to work for me."

"No one can know if a new position is going to work in only a few weeks. There's an adjustment period. Six months."

"I'll know. Six weeks," she countered back.

"Four months and not a minute less."

Claire heard the underlying note in his voice that meant he was done negotiating. She eyed him and then sighed, "Fine. Four months. Starting right away."

"Very well. If at the end of those four months, you decide the childcare center is not for you, I will personally guarantee you a position elsewhere in the company."

"What if I don't want to be in Chicago after those four months?" she asked, wondering how much he was willing to give.

"We'll cross that bridge when and if we come to it."

Claire nodded. "Fine."

Travis stood back up and headed for the door. "I'll drive. What time do we need to leave?"

"No later than eight o'clock."

"I'll be here then. The weather is supposed to continue to clear off tomorrow, so the roads should be much easier to navigate."

"I can drive…"

"No, I'll drive. You can be the navigator," Travis told her with a smile.

Claire's heart stopped at those words, and she struggled against reacting to them. She nodded, dropping her chin to her chest when her vision clouded with tears. A hand touched her hair a moment later; Travis had come back.

"Claire?"

She waved him off and inhaled deeply before slowly releasing the breath. Again, she filled her lungs, willing the emotional pain away.

"I'm fine. It's just…Scott used to say those exact same words."

Travis sighed and squatted down next to her. "Claire, I want to help you, but I don't like knowing that everything I say has the potential to be a landmine."

Claire met his eyes and shook her head. "It's not your problem. I've just pushed those memories aside for so long…"

"It will get better with time. The more you choose to remember, the easier it will be when something triggers a memory. I promise."

"Is that what worked for you?" she asked softly.

"Yeah. I tried shutting the past out after Emily passed away, but my family wouldn't let me. Oh, they gave me a few weeks and then they started casually making remarks about Emily and our life together. It hurt at first, but it does get better."

"I'll take your word for it." Claire took another breath and then gave him a watery smile, "Thank you for going with me on Monday. I'll be ready at eight on Monday."

"Are you sure you're okay?" Travis asked, standing up at the same time she did.

"I'm sure."

"Okay. You have my number. Don't hesitate to call me if you just need someone to talk to. I'm a pretty good listener."

Claire nodded and then walked him to the door. "Thank you, again."

Travis reached out a hand and brushed a stray strand of hair off her cheek. "You look more rested than a few days ago. We should have more snowstorms like this."

"You would be broke if the store had to stay closed too many days this close to Christmas."

"Maybe. I think Hammerstein's could weather another storm or two. Get some sleep, and I'll see you Monday morning."

He headed for the elevator, and Claire shut the door. She was filled with a sense of relief that she wouldn't be returning to her past all alone. Although Travis was someone she'd just met, she'd shared more with him in the last few days than with anyone else in her adult life since Scott's death. He understood her, and when he'd touched her cheek a few moments earlier, she'd had the strangest urge to feel his arms wrapped around her. She'd missed physical interaction with another human being.

She told herself that she wasn't really attracted to Travis. It was simply the opportunity he presented to interact with another human being on a more personal level. The fact that his touch had sent tingles all the way down to her toes was irrelevant. She wasn't looking for a romantic interest, and he didn't appear to want anything of the sort, either.

Friends. She and Travis could be friends and co-workers. If spending some more time with him helped her get past some of the hurt she'd been hiding, she would be grateful.

Friends. Everyone needs a friend now and again, and Claire was no exception.

Chapter 8

Monday morning…

Travis glanced at the clock on the dashboard, wishing traffic would get moving so that he wouldn't be late picking Claire up. He'd personally dropped Tyler off at his preschool this morning, taking an extra few minutes to wander through the various rooms. Almost immediately, he'd spotted things he wanted to do differently with the one they were creating. They were just little things here and there, but Travis didn't believe in doing anything halfway. He preferred it close to perfect from the beginning.

He finally saw Claire's apartment complex up ahead and breathed a sigh of relief. He had two minutes to spare. He quickly pulled the luxury SUV into the short-term parking. He got out of the vehicle and came around the front, then stopped and watched as Claire exited the building. She'd evidently been waiting for him. She was bundled up against the wind which, no matter the season, was a constant companion of the city. Winter time was the worst in Travis' opinion; the frigid wind cut right through a person like icy shards of glass.

"Good morning," he told her, hurrying to open the passenger door and then shutting it just as quickly and jogging around to his own door. He wished he hadn't left his coat lying on the back seat. "Brrr. It's cold outside!"

"Where is your coat?" she asked, removing her gloves and fastening the seatbelt.

Travis tipped his head toward the backseat. "I took it off after taking Tyler to preschool. That might have been a bit premature. How are you this morning?"

Claire shrugged. "To be honest, I'm nervous. I almost called you and cancelled this trip several times this morning."

Travis put on his signal and then pulled back out into traffic. "Did you live in Winchester long?"

Claire was quiet for so long that he looked over at her and raised a brow. She nodded. "I was born there. So was Scott, my late husband."

Travis nodded and let that information process for a few minutes. No wonder she was nervous. She was going back to her hometown, but instead of it being a place of refuge in her darkest hours, she'd chosen to run away. Why? What was he missing here? Her husband had died, but he didn't know any of the details and he'd been reluctant to press her for any. He liked Claire. For some reason, he wanted to protect her and make everything right in her world.

He'd reasoned that her reaction to Tyler was due to the fact that she'd given up her love for working with young children after her husband's death. Being around his son must be a painful reminder of that time in her life. He hoped, as time went by and she began working with and around young children again, her grief would begin to lessen.

Travis had a natural inclination to act the protector, but what he felt for Claire was more than he could explain. He'd tried to chalk it up to them having shared a tragic loss, but even that didn't seem to be explanation enough. Instead of pressing her for answers while she was all tensed up with worry, he smiled and then turned on the radio.

Christmas music filled the inside of the car and he felt, rather than saw, Claire tense up even further. He lowered the volume and asked, "Do you have a problem with Christmas music? I mean, the Chipmunks aren't for everyone, but I've never met anyone who didn't like Bing Crosby."

Claire gripped her hands together, as she answered, "I'm not fond of Christmas music."

"Really? I would think a preschool teacher would be overly enthusiastic about the man in the red suit and reindeer."

"I'm not overly fond of anything to do with Christmas."

Travis frowned, and she turned her attention to the landscape outside the window. He watched her off and on for the next thirty minutes of silence, still getting the feeling that there was more going on here than she'd told him. As they approached the interchange between Interstate 90 and 65, Travis broke the silence, "Which way do you normally go?"

"There is no normally. I haven't been back to Winchester since I left. I went through Fort Wayne that time," she answered softly. "The traffic around Indianapolis is horrible no matter what time of day you get there. Fort Wayne seemed a bit easier to navigate."

"Then that's the way we'll go." He took the appropriate direction and soon they were driving along Interstate 90, heading toward Interstate 80. "I haven't been this direction in years."

"I'm surprised Douglas isn't driving you today," Claire told him.

"If I was traveling for work, he probably would be. I get a lot of work done while traveling if I don't have to do the driving."

"Is that why you have a chauffeur?" she asked, turning toward him slightly.

"Mostly. Also, Douglas is a personal friend who just happens to work with me. He's been helping me with Tyler from the moment he was born, first with my wife, and now. Frankly, I don't know that

I could function without him."

"It's nice that you have someone around to depend on," Claire murmured.

"Who did you depend on when your husband died?" Travis asked, longing to learn more about the beautiful woman sitting next to him.

"No one. His mother was still alive, but she was in the last stages of Alzheimer's and being taken care of in a special care center forty miles away."

"Surely friends…," he broke off when she hid a yawn and then turned even more toward the window. It was plain to see that his questioning was bothering her. Given the dark circles beneath her eyes, she was also fighting exhaustion. "Never mind. We have several hours of driving. Why don't you try to get some sleep?"

"I didn't sleep well last night."

"You'll sleep better tonight after we get back. Are you warm enough?" Travis inquired, fiddling with the heat on the passenger side of the vehicle. He turned it up to seventy-two and then suggested, "Use the controls on the bottom of your seat to lean back and get comfortable. I'll wake you up when we get to Fort Wayne, if you like."

"That will work."

Travis kept tabs on her as he drove, aware of when she finally relaxed enough to fall into a deep sleep. She snored softly and Travis bit back a smile, wondering how she would feel knowing that he'd heard her. Guessing she wouldn't thank him for mentioning it, he pushed it to the back of his mind and drove on.

***

Three hours later…

"Claire."

She heard someone calling her name, but it was the hand on her shoulder, gently shaking her that brought her awake. The sun was shining in the window of the car.

Car? Oh, I'm in Travis' car.

She turned her head to see him leaning toward her with a smile on his handsome face. "Are we in Fort Wayne?"

"Just about. I decided to stop and fuel up outside the city so that we didn't waste unnecessary time with the traffic. We can take the loop around the city and avoid most of the traffic."

"Okay. What time is it?"

"A little after eleven. We have another fifty minutes or so to drive and then we should be there. I'm going to step out and get fuel. Do you want something to drink or a chance to stretch your legs?"

Claire nodded and unfastened her seatbelt. She opened the car door and immediately closed it, reaching for her coat as her teeth chattered. Travis laughed behind her and she turned a mock glare his direction, "It's really cold outside."

"I know. That's why I have my coat on. Something I see you've just remembered you took off."

Claire nodded and shoved her arms into her coat, fighting to get it pulled down in the confines of the car. When that proved more hassle than it was worth, she opened the car door and then dashed for the store, yanking down her coat as she ran. Travis' laughter followed her, and she was surprised to feel herself smiling as she reached the glass door and pulled it open.

"Looks like you're a might cold there," the attendant, an elderly man with white hair and a beard, called to her.

"I won't be warm again until springtime," she called back, as she headed for the ladies' room.

Claire took care of her personal needs and then headed back out to the vehicle. Travis was just finishing up the fueling process and he immediately climbed back into the driver's seat and started the car, turning the heater on high.

Claire appreciated the warm air. Within a few minutes, they were both feeling much warmer. She looked over at Travis, as he pulled them back out onto the highway and she murmured softly, "In case I forget to say this later today, thank you."

Travis glanced at her and then reached over and smoothed a strand of hair back behind her ear. "You don't have to thank me."

Claire swallowed around the tingling sensation his light touch caused and resisted the urge to turn her head into his hand. "I'm sure you had plenty of other things you could be doing today."

"That's the beauty of being the boss, I get to decide for the most part what those things are going to be."

Claire nodded. "Thank you anyway."

"Are you excited to see your hometown again?"

"To be honest, I'm terrified. Four years ago, I walked away from everything there. It was a really bad time in my life. I just needed space to breathe. At least, that's how I justified it at the time."

"You have no family still living there?"

"None. My parents were only children, as was I. They died several years before my husband. Scott's parents had him late in life, and his mom was the only one still alive when he passed away. She didn't remember him most of the time. She passed away several months after I moved to the city."

"I'm sorry. That sounds very lonely."

"I'm used to it."

Travis didn't like the way she sounded so resigned to her life remaining that way. "Well, I'm putting you on notice to hang on because your life is about to change. For the better, I hope."

Claire gave him a wary look. When he simply smiled at her, she turned her attention back to the landscape. Travis allowed her to withdraw from their conversation. She was going to have enough stress to deal with in just under thirty minutes. He stowed his additional questions aside for now.

Chapter 9

Winchester, Indiana...

Claire looked at the familiar façade of the building she'd called her second home for so many years after college. The building had been purchased with her parent's life insurance money. When she'd agreed to sell the business to Shelly, she'd left the purchase price and all of the legal paperwork to the accountants, lawyers, and Shelly.

"Ready to go inside?" Travis asked, turning the vehicle off and pocketing the keys.

Claire nodded and then forced herself to open the car door. She pulled her coat around herself, like armor, and began to walk up the sidewalk. They had been shoveled that morning and piles of fresh snow lie on either side of the wet concrete. Some sort of snowmelt product had been sprinkled over the surface, ensuring ice wouldn't be forming anytime soon.

She reached the front doors, but before she could reach for the handle, Travis reached across her shoulder and did the honors himself.

"Thank you," she murmured as she preceded him into the building.

A squeal and the sound of her name being called out cheerfully told her she hadn't arrived unnoticed. "Claire!"

She turned and watched as Shelly, a very large and very pregnant Shelly, hustled toward her. "Shelly?" Claire eyed her bulging belly. "Should you be up on your feet?" The woman looked as if she was going to deliver any minute.

"Oh, I'm not due for another three weeks." Shelly wrapped Claire in an awkward hug. "Welcome home."

"Thanks," Claire murmured, turning to find Travis. "Shelly, this is Travis Hammerstein."

"Mr. Hammerstein, we spoke just last week." Shelly released Claire and then shook hands with Travis.

"That we did. Nice to meet you in person."

Shelly beamed a smile at him and then grabbed Claire's arm, "Come to the office. I brought your boxes out of storage this morning."

"Boxes?" Claire questioned.

"Oh, I saved everything," Shelly told her with a giggle. "I think there's fifteen of them."

Travis leaned forward and whispered in her ear, "Fifteen boxes are not going to fit in the vehicle we drove down."

Claire gave him a puzzled look, "I didn't know she saved everything. I thought maybe it was just my license and a few things here and there."

Travis grinned at her. "Guess you had someone looking out for you here after all."

"Here we are," Shelly declared, waiting on them to catch up to her. "I've redone the carpeting, but everything else is pretty much the same."

Claire paused at the doorway and nodded. Shelly wasn't joking when she said it looked the same. The only thing missing were Claire's personal effects, pictures of her family, the little potted succulents she'd remembered to water once a week, and the snow globe collection that had occupied the upper shelf of her office. All of that was gone now, and she buried the sense of regret that brought unwanted tears to her eyes.

"It looks very organized."

"Thanks. Come on in. The boxes are there in the corner. I thought about moving them for you, but I wanted to make sure I got a chance to see you when you came home."

Claire stepped into the office and stopped still in her tracks. The entire corner of the office was filled with oversized plastic boxes. She'd been expecting small file boxes or something similar, but these boxes were three times that size. "All of that is mine?"

Shelly smiled, proud of herself. "I carefully wrapped up all of the breakable stuff, and I marked the boxes so that you would know what was in each one of them."

Claire walked over to the stack of plastic tubs, aware that Travis was close behind her. "I can't believe she did all of this."

Travis read the label on the box closest to himself and then lifted the lid off. Inside, wrapped in brown newspaper, was the beloved snow globe collection Claire had been adding to since she was a little girl. She watched as Travis carefully unwrapped the globe on top, revealing the tiny replica of the North Pole.

He held it up for her to see and shook it so that the glitter inside swirled around and rained down on the small figurine inside, giving the appearance that it was snowing inside the glass orb. "Santa's Village?"

"North Pole," Claire corrected him. She reached for another globe, opening it up to reveal Santa's sleigh and the reindeer in flight. She'd never quite figured out how they'd gotten the figurine to stay suspended, and it had been one of her favorites in the collection.

She turned to Shelly with tears in her eyes. "I can't believe you've been storing this stuff for four years."

"It wasn't mine to throw away, and we always hoped you'd come home one day."

"We?" Claire asked, having heard Shelly refer to more than one person multiple times now.

"Sure," Shelly nodded. "A bunch of us helped. In fact, you should stop by the police station and see Jim after you leave here."

"Jim is still on patrol?" Claire asked, lifting the lid off of another box and finding all of her books and other learning resources carefully stacked inside.

"Jim is, but Marie got married and quit the force last year. She and Tim Dawson—you remember the Dawson's? They owned the hardware store."

"I remember," Claire nodded.

"Well, she and Tim got married and then a few months later she found out she was pregnant with triplets. She quit and is a stay-at-home mom now."

"Triplets?" Claire shook her head, "I can't even imagine."

"Yeah, everyone in town has been helping them out. The older ladies take turns going over in the mornings to help her get the babies fed and bathed, and they help her clean, do the laundry, get dinner cooking…basically, whatever Marie needs help with."

"That's really nice of them."

Shelly gave her a curious look and then shook it away and continued, "The teenagers show up after school and take care of the yard work, stringing Christmas lights, whatever else needs doing. Tim works until five and then he goes home and takes over until morning again."

"That's amazing," Claire commented.

"Oh, the schedule was a lot more complex when they first brought the babies home. The townsfolk were taking turns staying the night with them back then." Shelly's pager went off and after glancing at it, she scowled, "Drats. I need to go check this out. Take your time looking through everything. I wasn't sure what you wanted to do with all of this, since you said you live in Chicago now. Wow, I can't imagine you in the big city." Shelly grinned at her, "Go figure. Anyway, if you decide you want to have this stuff back there with you, I can help arrange to ship this and anything else you want to keep." Her pager went off again and she grimaced, "Gotta go. Are you in town for a while?"

"I was just planning for the day," Claire told her.

"Oh," Shelly's smile fell. "Well, I'm sure you'll be back more often now, and we can catch up then. Travis, it was nice to meet you. Claire, I think you'll like how everyone pitched in. See you guys later."

Claire gave a non-committal nod, replaying Shelly's words over in her head.

Why would she think that I would be coming back here more often? And why would I care if everyone pitched in? Maybe she was just scattered and rambling? She used to do that a lot when she got flustered.

Claire shook her head, dispelling the things that didn't make sense and then turned back to open another box. This one was filled with files, her framed license right on the top.

"Is that what you came here for?" Travis asked, looking over her shoulder, so close that she could feel his body heat. Rather than pulling away, she found herself resisting the urge to lean back and let her body rest against him.

What is wrong with me? He's not only my boss, but I've only known the man a few days!

"This is my license. The rest of this stuff... I don't even know where to begin," she looked over her shoulder at him helplessly.

"Is there a shipping place in town?"

"There used to be, next to the diner on Main Street."

"Well, I could eat so let's take care of two things at once."

Claire gave him an odd look and then pulled her license from the box before sealing it back up. "I should leave Shelly a note..."

"Give her your phone number, and you can call her once you have a shipping company lined up."

Claire nodded and jotted a quick note to her once friend, promising to be in contact soon about the other boxes. She left it taped to Shelly's door and then headed for the exit. Travis followed her, once again opening the doors for her. He opened the car door as well, and then set her license on the back seat.

Claire gave him directions to the center of town. She was pleasantly surprised to find a full-service shipping and moving company now occupied the space. She made arrangements to have the stuff in Shelly's office picked up and trucked to Chicago and then she and Travis headed for the diner.

It was very crowded, but Claire didn't let that bother her. She headed for a back booth, ignoring the curious stares and slight whispers that were occurring behind open hands. She recognized some people, so why shouldn't they return the favor.

"You're creating quite a stir," Travis murmured as his slid

into the booth opposite her.

"Just ignore them, not much excitement in this town on a weekday."

"Spoken from experience?" Travis asked.

"Yeah."

The waitress appeared next to their booth and pulled an order pad from her apron pocket and a pencil from behind her ear. Claire looked up and knew the minute Marjorie recognized her.

"Claire! Lord, child. It's good to see you."

Claire found herself pulled from the booth and wrapped in a warm hug. She returned the favor and then pulled away, "Hi, Marge."

"Child, why did you stay away so long? And who's this? Your new beau?"

Claire immediately shook her head, "No, Travis and I are just..."

"Friends," Travis supplied, shaking the other woman's hand."

"Actually, Travis is my boss and I just came down to get my childcare license."

"That's all? What about everything over at the house?"

"House? What are you talking about?" Claire asked.

Marjorie looked at her for a long moment and then shook her head, "No one told you."

"Told me what?"

"The house is still there."

94

"I assumed as much. I'm a little fuzzy on the details right now, but I believe it was sold for enough to pay off the mortgage."

Marjorie started laughing and then walked away, calling out to her husband Carl, who also served as the diner's line cook. "Carl, get out from behind that window and come say hello to Claire."

"Claire's back? Yay! I'm coming. Don't you dare let her leave."

Travis watched the commotion and then asked, "Still doing okay?"

"No. I feel kind of like I've fallen into an episode of the *Twilight Zone*."

Travis smiled as Carl and Marjorie returned. "See, I told you it was her."

"Girly, you've been missed," Carl told her, pulling her in for a big bear hug. Carl and Marjorie had been best friends with her parents and had been frequent visitors to her childhood home while she was growing up. She'd always considered them a sort of surrogate grandparents and receiving one of Carl's famous bear hugs felt much nicer than she'd imagined. It felt familiar and comforting. Both things she'd been missing these last four years.

Claire's mind was spinning. "It's nice to see you, as well."

"Carl, she doesn't know about the house," Marjorie elbowed her husband.

Carl's eyebrows disappeared beneath his hairline and he shook his head, "Figures George Watson wouldn't get that right. He's passed on now, God rest his soul, or I'd haul him over here and make him explain things right and proper. Well," Carl untied his apron and tossed it toward the empty countertop. "I guess Marjorie and I will just have to muddle our way through things. I don't

95

imagine you folks want to stay and eat right now?"

Claire shook her head, "Show me what you're talking about."

"Fair enough. Take her to her house. The missus and I will meet you there."

Travis nodded and then escorted Claire back out to the vehicle. "Any idea of what they're talking about?"

"Not a clue. Winchester is the most mundane town around, so why do I feel as if I've fallen into an alternate dimension?"

"How about I tell the shippers to hold off until we get back to them?" Travis suggested.

Claire nodded, so grateful that Travis had come with her today. Whatever she was about to find out, no doubt, was going to throw her into an emotional tailspin. Finding out that Shelly had kept all of her things had already rocked the steady foundation she thought she'd built up, and now it looked like the protective walls she'd created were about to be knocked down as well.

Travis opened the passenger door and then waited until she was seated before replying. "Is it possible that maybe the people in this town were supporting you and, in your grief, you were blind to it?"

Claire looked at him and then shrugged, confusion on her face. "I don't know."

"Well, let's go find out," Travis told her, shutting the door and then walking into the shipping office. After only a few minutes, he returned, jogging around the front and climbing behind the wheel. "They're going to hold off on picking your things up from the preschool. I told them we'd get back to them this afternoon.

"So, where am I going?"

Claire gave him directions to the house she'd thought to never see again. Her instructions to the real estate agent and lawyer had been to sell the house, pay off the mortgage and then donate the rest of the money to a needy cause. She'd signed a power of attorney over for everything, making George Watson, one of the town's only lawyers at the time, her representative in matters related to Winchester. She hadn't realized the man had died and wondered what it was that he'd done. Once again, she was plagued by a wave of guilt that she'd just walked away. She should know what had become of the home she'd shared with Scott. And their things. She should know about those things, but she didn't. Hadn't wanted to until just a few moments ago.

When Travis made the last turn, heading for the two-story ranch house at the end of the street, Claire realized she was holding her breath.

"Breathe," Travis whispered quietly to her as he slowed down. "Someone's been taking very good care of the landscaping. It's gorgeous."

"It's grown up quite a bit since I left." She looked to the side of the garage, where Scott had built Daniel a small playset and planted several fruit trees. The trees had only been five or six feet tall at the time of their deaths, and now they rose up toward the top of the roof.

Travis pulled into the circular driveway and then came to a stop, adjacent to the bright red front doors. "Were the doors red when you lived here before?" he asked.

Claire nodded and then undid her seatbelt. "Scott read somewhere that a red front door meant the house was a place full of energy, life and excitement. I guess there are a lot of meanings, but he liked the idea that the front door was the portal to the home within. The Chinese believe a red front door is lucky, and during the

97

Underground Railroad days, a red front door indicated it was a safe place for the travelers to rest."

"That's a lot of information about red front doors."

"Scott like to learn new things," she murmured, opening the door to exit the vehicle. She waited until Travis joined her before she stepped out from behind the door and took a hesitant step toward the structure. "I…"

Travis reached for her hand, clasping it firmly between his own. "You can do this. We'll go up and meet the new owners and see whatever Carl and Marjorie wanted you to see."

Claire took a deep breath and then nodded. "If nobody's home, I can always send a letter wishing them well."

"Yes, you could do that." Travis and she began their walk to the front doors, when the sound of an approaching truck stopped them. "There's Carl and his wife. Want to wait for them?"

"Yes. Maybe they already know who lives here now and can introduce us?" Claire told him, keeping her eyes on the truck that had now stopped directly behind Travis's.

"Sorry about the delay, folks," Carl said as he exited the truck. "Decided I'd better stop by and get a key."

"Key?" Claire asked.

"To the house, hon," Marjorie told her with a smile. "Well, go on and get the door open Carl. I imagine she's anxious to see everything."

Claire stared at the older couple and shook her head, "I don't understand."

"What is there to understand?"

"Why do you have a key to this house? Are you watching it

for the new owners? I don't want to trespass."

"New owners? Lordy, hon. Did you and George never talk?"

"Not after I left here," Claire admitted. "I signed a power of attorney, so there was no need for me to."

"Well, I'll be. This is a pickle, isn't it," Carl exclaimed. He shook his head and then nodded to his wife, "Best grab her arm and hold on tight. Don't want her passing out on us."

Marjorie stepped close and looped an arm around Claire's shoulders. "Come on inside, hon and Carl and I will try out best to explain things."

Claire resisted Marjorie's attempt to pull her forward. "Wait. I don't need to go inside. I can wait until whoever lives here now gets home."

Travis stepped closer to her and added, "I think what Claire is trying to say is that she doesn't need to go inside to know that whoever lives here now has taken great care of the place."

"The entire town helps out with that," Carl informed them before turning and heading for the front door.

"Why would the entire town help out with the maintenance on this house?" Travis asked, turning to Marjorie for the answer.

She looked between Travis and Claire. "Claire, hon, this is your house."

Chapter 10

Claire heard the words, but they didn't make any sense. She looked at Marjorie and when the older woman nodded, Claire felt her knees buckle. She was glad when Travis caught her, holding her up until she was able to stand on her own again.

"My house? No," she shook her head. "I had the real estate agent put it on the market."

"He didn't," Marjorie confirmed.

"Why not? Oh goodness, what about the mortgage?"

"Well, now. It seems your husband had an insurance policy on himself that was large enough to cover the remaining principal on the mortgage. There was no need to sell the house."

"No need? I don't understand," Claire murmured, stopping as dizziness clouded her vision. When she started to sway, Travis was there with a supportive arm. She didn't even consider not leaning against Travis's side. He became her anchor point as the world she'd thought she knew was suddenly tipped sideways and spun around like a top.

Carl came back out of the house and tried to explain, "George called a town meeting about a week after you left. It was decided that you were suffering and needed our help, whether you wanted it or not. We always hoped you come back home once you'd dealt with your sorrow…"

"We never thought it would take years, though," Marjorie commented, adding to the guilt Claire was feeling.

These people had taken on the responsibility of caring for her things, hoping she'd eventually heal and come home. What they didn't know was that she'd been hiding in the city, doing the exact opposite of healing. She'd been ignoring what had happened in an effort to minimize the pain.

Now, staring her in the face, was the result of her decision. A past that was no longer in the past and still had to be dealt with. Her head swam with the implications of what Carl and Marjorie were telling her.

I still own this house. That means all of our stuff is still inside.

Claire swallowed audibly and then took a hesitant step toward the open doors. She took another, feeling Travis moving with her, grateful for his support. When she reached the front step, she paused for a moment and then looked up at him.

"I think I need to do this on my own," she spoke so softly she wasn't sure he'd heard her until he squeezed her shoulder and then dropped his arm away from her. He took a step back, and Carl moved down to the sidewalk, giving her an unobstructed path into what had once been a place of refuge and happiness. Claire looked at the door and then finished taking the steps needed to place her in the foyer, inside the house.

She was assaulted by memories as she looked around the space. Nothing had really changed. It was all clean and organized. The Christmas decorations no longer held court on the mantle or on the bookshelves, and the tree had been removed. She would guess it was packed away in the garage. She wandered into the family room, skimming her fingertips along framed pictures, small treasures that held so many memories.

Tears flowed freely down her cheeks as she wandered through the first floor. Everywhere she looked, she saw another physical reminder of the past. Each one carried a special memory. She was overcome with gratitude and guilt for ever thinking she needed to give this all up. She'd only started to regret her exit strategy from Winchester after starting to talk about the past with Travis. She'd mourned the loss of things and special gifts and suddenly having them all returned to her was a miracle she could barely process.

***

Hope hovered over Claire as her charge walked through her memories. She was pleased to find that most of the memories were fun-filled and happy. The pictures told a similar story. Hope couldn't contain the grin that spread across her face at the gift Claire had been given by the town. They'd salvaged something so precious, and all with the intent of restoring it to Claire when the time was right.

She watched as Travis slowly stepped into the house twenty minutes later, softly calling Claire's name.

She was standing in the kitchen and walked to meet him, tears still flowing unchecked down her cheeks. "I can't believe they did this."

Travis smiled tenderly at her and then used his thumbs to try and wipe her tears away. "Are these happy or sad?"

"Overwhelmed?" Claire replied, turning and eyeing the staircase. She hadn't yet been up to visit the bedrooms and part of her was now dreading to do so. Travis saw what caught her attention. Hope waited to see what he would do. After only a momentary pause, she got the answer she'd been praying for.

"Want me to go up with you?"

Claire nodded and slowly climbed the stairs. She turned left at the landing, pushing open the first door and stepping into what was obviously the master suite. A large canopy bed took up residence against the far wall. She slowly walked into the room and toward the walk-through closet. She stopped in her tracks when she saw her clothing hanging there just like the day...

She forced that bad thought away and turned, frowning when she saw Scott's side of the closet was completely empty. Rather than soul-wrenching grief, now she only felt a sad recognition that even though the house was still as she remembered it, her life could never return to the way it had been before. It just wasn't possible.

She sighed and then turned around and walked out of the closet and out of the room. She crossed the landing to the first door on the right and her hand hovered over the knob. When she didn't turn the knob, Travis reached around her and completed the task, pushing the door slightly ajar.

Claire peeked through the crack to see the bright blue walls she'd painted before attaching the vinyl dinosaur decals to the walls. Daniel had loved dinosaurs above all other animals, and she'd taken great joy in creating a bedroom just for him.

She pushed the door completely open and then frowned at the blank walls. The dinosaur decals had been removed, as had the children's toys that had once stood in the corner. She walked over and opened up the dresser drawers, once again finding them empty. A noise behind her spun her around.

Travis was looking at the room and then her, his face a mixture of sudden understanding. "You had a little boy?"

Claire nodded, "Daniel. He was injured the same night Scott was shot."

"Shot?" Travis walked to her and pulled her into his arms, ignoring how her body stiffened. He held fast until she relaxed and gave into the comfort he was offering. "You never explained..."

"I couldn't. They went out to do some last-minute Christmas shopping. There was an incident at the mall. Daniel was shot and killed instantly, or so they said. Daniel was also shot. They rushed him to the children's hospital in Indianapolis. He died a couple days later."

Claire's voice sounded monotone and so impersonal to her own ears. Travis didn't seem to mind. He simply stood there, holding her against his chest and giving her his warmth and support.

"How old was he?"

"Four."

"No wonder you reacted the way you did to Tyler."

"They look a little alike. When he first approached me, I thought it was Daniel and I freaked out."

"Maybe just a little freak," Travis agreed, pulling back and smiling down into her eyes. He watched her for a moment and then looked around the room. "I'm guessing the walls weren't bare before?"

Claire shook her head and then extricated herself from his arms. She walked over to the closet and frowned at the stack of marked boxes inside. A noise behind her had her spinning around to see Marjorie standing in the doorway, worrying her hands in front of her.

"We packed away all of Scott and Daniel's things. Some people wanted to donate them, but others of us thought you should get to make that decision."

Claire nodded and then shut the closet door. "Thank you."

"No thanks are necessary, hon." Marjorie nodded at her and turned to leave. She took a few steps and then paused, meeting Claire's eyes as she nodded toward the other bedroom down the hallway. "I personally took care of that room. I'm really sorry, hon. Most of us didn't know…

Claire shook her head and then met the other woman's eyes. "You couldn't have."

Marjorie nodded and then left them alone once again. Claire stared after her, knowing she needed to go look in the other bedroom. It was the last part of the bandage that needed to be ripped off, but the hardest for her to bear. She'd felt guilty for Scott and Daniel's deaths, but in reality, she knew she hadn't been the one to pull the trigger. The third death…well, that was on her. She'd allowed her grief and concern for Daniel to overshadow the fact that she had a precious little life growing inside of her that needed her protection. She'd failed her unborn child and that hurt as much or more because the guilt was all hers to bear.

"What was Marjorie talking about?" Travis asked quietly.

Claire glanced at him and then walked from the room and down the hallway. She didn't hesitate to open the door this time, needing a quick ripping away of the shroud she'd been living behind. The yellow painted walls had already existed before she'd rearranged the room, bringing the crib in from the garage and moving the rocking chair into the corner. She'd set up the nursey, intending to bring Scott here after putting Daniel down to bed that night. She'd known he would be ecstatic about the new addition to their family. She'd wanted to share that knowledge with him as Christmas Day had arrived.

Because she'd chosen to keep that knowledge from him for two weeks, he'd died not knowing he was going to be a father again; another source of guilt she had to live with. A fresh wave of tears overtook her, and she sank to the floor in the middle of the room, wrapping her arms around her middle.

"I'm so sorry," she whispered brokenly to the room.

Chapter 11

Travis watched Claire leave what had been her little boy's room, and he took a moment to get a handle on his own emotions. When the reality of the loss she'd suffered had finally revealed itself, it had been like a punch to his gut. Tyler was his whole world, and while losing Emily had been horrible, losing Tyler would be devastating. He wasn't even sure if he would be able to recover from that sort of loss. Yet, Claire had been dealt a double blow.

No wonder she's been trying to avoid dealing with this. I'm not so sure I wouldn't have done the same thing.

He took several calming breaths, wanting to be strong for her. She'd already been nervous about this trip. Then, to find out that everything she'd left behind was right here waiting for her to return...well, he could tell by looking at her face that she was on overload.

A horrible cry of pain, so filled with anguish that it made him ache inside, came from somewhere else. He rushed from the room and searched the hallway for the direction it had come. When it came again, he followed the sound to the end of the hall and stopped at the sight of Claire doubled over on the floor in the middle of what was obviously meant as a nursery.

She was sobbing uncontrollably and apologizing, but he didn't know to whom or for what. Tears filled his eyes. He went to her, sinking to the floor and pulling her physically into his lap.

"Claire, shush. It's going to be alright. I'm here."

"It will never be alright," she cried, burying her face against his shoulder and holding onto him as if he was her lifeline.

Travis wrapped his arms around her tighter and then looked

at Marjorie and Carl, who had rushed up the stairs when they'd heard her first cry out.

"Is she okay?" Marjorie whispered.

Travis shook his head, "No, but she will be."

"Why don't you bring her downstairs?" Marjorie suggested. "I think I'll call the doctor as well and ask him to stop by."

Travis nodded and then slid Claire off his lap. She reluctantly let go, so he was able to stand to his feet. He lifted her by the shoulders and then swung her up into his arms and carried her out of the nursery and down the stairs, depositing them both on the couch.

He could hear Marjorie bustling around in the kitchen and heard the low tenor of Carl's voice as he spoke to someone on the phone. They both joined him and Claire a few minutes later, but Claire just continued to cry in his arms. This was obviously something she'd needed to do for a long time. Travis was in no hurry to release her.

"Shhh," he murmured comforting words to her and rubbed one hand up and down her back in a soothing motion. After a while, her tears started to subside. She sat in his arms, her eyes closed, exhausted from her emotional outburst.

Travis could feel her body relaxing as sleep claimed her. Still, he continued to sit with her in his arms. When a soft knock sounded on the door, Carl answered it and returned with the doctor a few minutes later.

"I told him all that's happened today. Well...the parts I knew about," Carl explained in a whisper.

"Is she sleeping?" The doctor asked.

"I think so. She cried herself out."

The doctor nodded and then withdrew a stethoscope from his bag and approached Travis and Claire. He listened to her heartbeat. Claire never moved or blinked in recognition of his arrival.

"Everything sounds fine. Maybe I'll just have a cup of tea and wait until she wakes up. I would have thought she would have dealt with her grief by now, but she always was a stubborn little girl."

Travis said nothing, not wanting to debate whether or not Claire had handled the deaths of her husband and children the correct way. Children. Plural. Not just her little boy. Given what he'd quickly pieced together, she'd been pregnant at the time of their death. Having dealt with a small portion of a similar grief, there was no right or wrong way. It was just there. Each individual person had to handle things and process their emotions on their own terms.

How long he sat there, he couldn't have said. Some time later, he felt her stir in his arms and he looked down to see her watching him with eyes that held no happiness. "Hey."

"How long have you been holding me?" She asked, her voice scratchy from her crying spell.

"Don't know. Don't care. The doctor's here."

She turned her head and frowned at the kitchen. "Dr. Pattison?"

Travis nodded. "Marjorie called him. You were pretty upset."

Claire swallowed and nodded, "Yeah. Guess trying to keep from dealing with things didn't work out quite the way I envisioned."

"It never does. Wanna talk about anything?"

Claire shook her head and then sat up and scooted off his lap until she was sitting on the couch beside him. "Not really. I guess you figured everything out?"

"I think so. You don't have to talk now. At some point, and with someone, you need to start talking about the past. Believe me, it really does help."

"I will. I'm just a little raw right now. I can't believe they kept my house and everything in it."

"The people in this town are pretty special," Travis told her.

"I guess I never realized that until just now. Gosh, what time is it?"

"Almost four o'clock."

"What? Oh, Travis. I'm sorry. We should head back. Tyler's going to be missing his daddy."

"Well, actually, while you were sleeping I kind of rearranged our plans."

Claire raised a brow and asked, "How?"

"Douglas is bringing Tyler here, along with a moving truck. I don't know what all you might want to keep, if anything…or maybe you want to keep everything, but I wanted you to have the option to take some things back to Chicago with you."

Claire only stared at him. Travis was afraid he'd overstepped his bounds, but then she smiled. "That's the sweetest thing I think anyone has ever done for me. Thank you. I would love to have some things back in Chicago with me. As for the house…I never dreamed I still owned it. I really can't see myself coming back to live here."

"And you don't have to make that decision today or even next week. You've been given a do-over that most people never get.

Take your time and, when it feels right, then you can make a decision."

Claire nodded, and he watched her shoulders relax. "I should go talk to Dr. Pattison."

"He was concerned about you."

"He would be. He's been the doctor in Winchester since shortly after I was born. He delivered Daniel and most of the other babies born in this town."

"Sounds like a small-town doctor."

"Yeah. He has help now and, with the small county hospital just a mile out of town, he's able to treat more people here without having to send them to the city."

"Well, he seemed concerned about you, as are Marjorie and Carl."

"I should apologize for worrying them," Claire murmured.

"Don't you dare apologize for feeling true emotion," Travis told her. "You feel what you feel, and others can either deal with it or stay away."

"That's a pretty hardline approach."

"Yeah, but it works. Trying to hide how you really feel to save others from having to feel anything is bogus and doesn't do you any good. It's time for you to start doing what's healthy for you. Everyone else can either deal or leave."

Claire smiled at him and nodded, "Message received loud and clear."

"Good."

Claire nodded and then stood up to head for the kitchen and

the sound of the other's voices. Travis watched her go and then sent a message to Douglas. He'd picked Tyler up from school two hours ago and they were headed to procure a moving truck and then begin their journey here. They would need to spend the night. If Claire wasn't comfortable staying in her house, they'd get hotel rooms in town or somewhere close by. Whatever she needed, that was what Travis was going to supply.

Chapter 12

Guardian Angel School

Hope entered the schoolroom, pleased to see Matthias standing at one of the windows. Usually she had to go track him down and, after watching Claire's emotional eruption, she just wanted some reassurance that the plan that had come to mind would work. She was also hoping that, by discussing it with Matthias first, he'd give his approval, so she wouldn't have to wonder if she was breaking any of the rules.

"Hope, come join me," Matthias called out without turning around.

"How did you know it was me?" Hope asked, coming to a stop beside him. She looked out the window and smiled, as she watched the animals playing with one another in the field beyond. On earth, these animals would have been mortal enemies. Here in the Heavenly realms, everyone and everything got along with one another.

"What brings you looking for me this day?" Matthias asked, glancing at her sideways.

"Well, I've just come from Claire's hometown. She's finally opening up and dealing with the grief of losing her family. It was heart wrenching to watch."

"Please tell me you didn't do anything to interfere with her emotions?" Matthias asked, turning to look at her fully now.

"No, no. I promise. I learned my lesson last year. I wouldn't do that. It was cathartic for her to cry and finally share, albeit not so much by choice but by circumstance, the fact that she'd lost her family."

Matthias looked at her a moment longer and then nodded, "I believe you. So, tell me what else is on your mind."

"She's suffering from guilt, along with grief and the other emotions that come along with losing a loved one."

Matthias frowned. "What is she feeling guilty about?"

"Well, see, here's the reason I came to see you. I had picked up that she was feeling guilty, but I thought it was more of the survivor's type. I lived and they didn't; that type of thing."

Matthias smiled at her choice of vocabulary, but Claire ignored him and continued. "Anyway, that's not it at all. No, she's feeling guilty because she kept the knowledge that she was pregnant to herself. Her husband died without knowing he was going to be a father for a second time."

"Ah," Matthias nodded slowly. "That is a different sort of guilt altogether. Also, a tough one to counteract. There's no way to bring her husband back so she can tell him. I don't recall seeing that she's started praying more frequently."

"I know that, but I was thinking…what if she could somehow be reassured that her husband knows about the baby and that everyone is up here where she wants them to be?"

"If you're going to suggest sending her to a medium and allowing them to try and contact her husband through the world…Don't!"

"I would never. You know things like that are frowned upon and the power for that comes from that other place. You know, the one down below."

"I know what you're referring to, and I'm aware of where that kind of power comes from. So, if you are not suggesting a séance, what exactly are you planning?"

"I was thinking about using a dream..."

"That is above your pay grade, Claire. Guardian angels do not have the power, or the authority, to influence human's dreams."

Claire shuffled her feet and then nodded, "I know that. I was kind of thinking maybe you could..."

"You're asking me to make an exception for you..."

"No! No, I don't want to be the one who gives her the dream. I was hoping you would."

Matthias opened his mouth to reply and then closed it just as quickly. "You want me to influence her dreams? In what way? I'm assuming you've already formulated what you'd like to see happen in this dream?"

Claire nodded. "I want her to see her husband with their little boy and the baby she never got to hold. I checked, and it was a little girl. Claire doesn't know that, and I think it would give her comfort to know that they are all together and that her husband is watching out for both children until she can join them."

Matthias was silent for a long time. Claire was almost positive he was going to deny her request. After almost ten minutes, he nodded once and then turned toward her. "When I was a guardian angel trainee, I had a charge who had lost his parents in a terrible train accident. He'd been sent away to a reform school because of his bad and rebellious behavior. His parents and his relationship had been very strained.

"Over the course of the school year, James had gotten his act together and had flourished at the school. He was receiving the highest marks for his grade. There was virtually no trace of the rebellious teenager who had first arrived on the steps of the school."

Matthias sighed. "He hadn't gone home for any of the school

breaks, not wanting to see the disappointment in his parents' eyes, but when graduation came around, he wrote and asked them to attend. They agreed, and he was looking forward to beginning a new chapter with both of them."

"They never made it to graduation, did they?" Hope asked quietly.

"No, you are correct. They never made it to the school to watch James graduate. He turned his grief to anger and became more rebellious than ever. He started taking risks and soon was openly challenging everyone and everything."

"In a bold move, I contacted his parents and asked them to speak to him through a dream. They agreed, sharing with him how proud they were of his progress and that they only wished they'd lived long enough to tell him in person how proud and excited they were for him to come back home to live."

"You let his parents speak to him in a dream?" Hope asked, her mind racing with ideas.

"Now, don't go getting any ideas, Claire. What I did broke almost a dozen rules. Luckily for me, it worked out and James got his act together for a second time. It helped to know that his parents were both in the ministry, so I was fairly certain they would say the correct thing. My point is, that situation could have gone very badly for James. Some humans put a lot of emphasis on their dreams."

"But, wouldn't it be worth a try? Maybe they wouldn't even have to say anything. If she could just get a glimpse of them in Heaven, the children with her late husband, being cared for and happy?"

Matthias pursed his lips and then nodded again, only a single time. "That would be the safest way to try this idea of yours. Now, you must not influence Claire's response to the dream or plant ideas

115

about what it means."

Hope nodded and thought about crossing her fingers behind her back, but that would be dishonest. Her shoulders sagged. "Fine."

"Cheer up, little angel. There's a silver lining here. I would say your charge is finally heading down the correct path. You still have almost a week before Christmas gets here. There's still hope that she'll remember how much she liked the holiday and want to celebrate it again."

"That's what I'm praying will happen for her. She's a really nice lady, and I hate seeing her so sad."

Matthias gave her an indulgent look, then nodded toward the doorway. "It looks like Charity is looking for someone. Might that be you?"

Hope turned and saw a fellow guardian angel in training looking in the schoolroom window. When Charity spotted her, she waved to her. Matthias let Hope know, "I would say that answers my question adequately enough. Go see what she likes, and I'll see what I can do about Claire's dream in the meantime."

"Thank you, Matthias."

Hope left the schoolroom and found Charity waiting for her. "Hi. What's up?"

"It's Joy. She's not feeling very joyful right now."

"Where is she?" Hope looked around the courtyard for her, but it was empty save for her and Charity.

"Down on Earth."

Hope smiled, "Let's go cheer her up."

Charity smiled back and they set off. Hope had a plan of attack for dealing with Claire, and while helping her, Travis had let go of some of his remaining depression, so she might well be on the way to helping him also. She needed to get back to Claire, but first she'd take a small detour to see if she could cheer up Joy. It was the Christmas season after all and being depressed about anything just wasn't right.

They found Joy sitting in a bank of dirty snow, her face a study in what being forlorn must look like.

"Joy," Hope called softly, as she and Charity came to a position on either side of her.

Joy turned around and shock flooded her face. "Hi! What are you two doing here?"

Hope shared a look with Charity and then explained, "We sensed that you were feeling a little lost. Is everything okay?"

"I thought so, but now…"

"Joy, you're not thinking of doing anything…illegal, are you?" Charity asked. As the most mature of the three, she often felt the need to adopt a motherly tone. Hope nodded, giving silent support to Charity's warning.

"No! Believe me, I learned my lesson last year." Joy had caused quite a stir when she'd dared to interfere with human emotions, and Matthias had been forced to step in to fix things.

Hope put an arm around Joy's shoulders. "We are all trying to do our very best. Have you talked to Matthias about whatever's not working?" Having just come from doing that, Hope knew their mentor was capable. He'd just proven how willing he was to lend a helping hand.

"Not yet."

"Maybe you should go do that instead of sitting here moping around. It's Christmas and no one, especially angels, should be moping in a pile of dirty, melted ice," Charity told her.

Joy looked down, and when she saw how dirty her gown had become, she gave both Hope and Charity a sheepish look. "Guess I should probably get cleaned up before I go see Matthias, huh?"

"I would strongly suggest that," Charity informed her with a smile.

Joy stood and gave the other two angels a confident nod. "I will figure this out. I just need to re-work my plan."

"With Matthias' help, right?" Hope inquired.

"Of course." Joy bid the other two angels farewell and then headed off.

Hope shared a smile with Charity. "Well, we did what we could. How are things going with your charge?"

Charity smiled, "Things are finally beginning to look up. It was touch and go there for a while. Today marks seven days where she hasn't spent most of the day at the cemetery. I was beginning to think she was going to set down roots and become a permanent fixture there."

"Grief does such strange things to humans, even when they know where their loved ones have gone," Hope added.

"Yes. That being said, I should really go check on her. Matthias told me there was a miracle coming but refused to tell me in what respect. He said it was better if I didn't know because then I would be tempted to break the rules, and he couldn't have that. Not on his watch."

"Miracles seem to be plentiful this time of year. One of my charges experienced a wonderful miracle today."

"One of your charges?" Charity asked. "I thought angels in training weren't allowed to have multiple charges?"

"We're not, but Matthias is bending the rules just a bit because my charges have a connection. While I was skeptical, they

118

seem to be helping one another overcome the events of the past that have been keeping them from moving forward and living fulfilled and happy lives."

"Good luck. I'll see you at choir practice?" Charity asked as she and Hope headed up into the air. Chicago was a long way from Denver by human standards, but for an angel, it was nothing. Hope would be there before Claire took her next breath.

"Choir practice it is." Hope waved and, in an instant, she was gone. There was less than a week until Christmas. This year, Hope wanted Claire to spend it with people who knew how to laugh and enjoy life. Both things she'd forgotten how to do over the last four years.

Chapter 13

Claire waved goodbye to the doctor one last time before she retreated back inside the place she'd once called home. She'd had a nice visit with Carl and Marjorie, and Dr. Pattison, assuring the latter that she wasn't on the verge of a mental breakdown; she just needed time to adjust to this latest turn of events.

Carl and Marjorie had left half an hour earlier. Now, she and Travis remained. Douglas and Tyler were still over an hour out. Claire wandered through the first floor of the house, a sense of detachment filling her for most of what she saw. She'd relegated these things to the past and had considered them gone. Now, she found out they'd been kept for her, but she wasn't sure she wanted most of it. Her life wasn't here any longer.

"What's that frown for?" Travis asked, walking into the room.

Claire turned and watched him. He was very handsome. Her heart skipped a beat when he smiled at her perusal.

"What?"

She shook her head, unable to voice the words. She turned back around and walked over to a large bookshelf. The contents were a mixture of both hers and Scotts, but anything she'd truly loved on the shelves, she'd already replaced. "I don't need or want most of this. I know that makes me sound ungrateful, but…"

"Don't worry so much about what others might think. You need to act in your best interest. If you don't want the things in this or any other room, then I'll help you find a buyer for them, or you can donate them to a worthy cause."

"I thought I already had," she murmured softly. She picked

up a book with worn corners and smiled. "This book was my mothers. She used to read it to me every night."

Travis joined her, looked at the book, and then asked, "Can you honestly say you're not happy to have it back in your possession?"

"No. I'll be forever grateful to whomever spearheaded the effort to keep this place up, but I don't need most of it."

"Douglas is bringing some boxes with him. He and I will help you pack up the things you do want to keep, and you can dispose of the rest."

Claire nodded and reached for another book. "That's a good idea. I'm sorry you had to cancel your plans."

"What plans? I had planned to convince you to have dinner with Tyler and me and then spend some more time going over the childcare center. From my perspective, this little change in plans works to my favor. I get to have dinner with you, and you can't say no."

Claire gave him a sad smile. "That actually sounds kind of pathetic."

Travis shared her smile. "Yeah, it does, but I'm going to take it for the win, anyway. Now, tell me honestly…how do you feel about sleeping in the house tonight?"

Claire looked up and then around the room. "There's really no reason to spend money on a hotel room…"

Travis reached out and laid a gentle finger over her lips. "I didn't ask you about money. I asked how you would feel sleeping under this roof."

He removed his finger and her lips tingled, but she resisted the urge to lift her hand up and rub at them. She cleared her throat instead and then answered, "I will be fine. I can sleep on the sofa down here. I don't think I could stand to sleep in the bedroom upstairs."

"You're not just saying that?" Travis asked, searching her eyes.

Claire shook her head. "No, we can stay here. I doubt I'll sleep much, anyway. There's a lot of stuff to go through."

"Tell me where you want to start. We can just make small piles in each room until Douglas arrives."

They spent the rest of the afternoon and well into the evening, going through drawers and closets. Claire set aside scrapbooks, a few knickknacks that had special significance for her, and then they reached her bedroom.

Douglas and Tyler had arrived and after retrieving several pizzas from the local shop in town, they'd been more than willing to pitch in and help pack. Daniel's bedroom had been easy enough to go through. All of his stuff had already been packed away in boxes. She'd pulled out the box containing his scrapbook and favorite items, but the rest was marked to be given away.

After Tyler fell asleep, Travis moved him to a pallet on the floor in the living room, all of them deciding that, for tonight, they would sleep downstairs. Douglas offered to stay with Tyler and finish packing up the items she'd set aside in the living room and kitchen, while Claire and Travis headed upstairs to tackle the master bedroom.

She started with her clothing, selected a few pieces, then did the same with her shoes. She'd taken all of her jewelry with her. Aside from a few items of Scott's which she pulled from one of the smaller boxes, there wasn't much else she was interested in keeping.

"I'm finished up here."

"Do you want to go through the other bedroom?" Travis inquired softly.

Claire inhaled deeply and glanced at the clock. She was surprised to see it was almost midnight. "There's not much in there yet."

"I'll finish up in here if you want to go get started"

Claire nodded and then walked to the last bedroom on the right. She stepped into the room, relieved when she wasn't bombarded with out-of-control emotions. The only things in the room that she was interested in keeping had been placed in the top drawer. A picture of the baby's ultrasound and a small rattle she'd purchased the day she'd decided to keep the baby a secret until Christmas Eve.

Another wave of guilt hit her, but she pushed it away this time. Travis was right. She hadn't intentionally set out to hurt Scott by keeping the news of their baby to herself. Using the knowledge as a gift, she'd been planning to surprise him. It wasn't her fault that fate had acted before she could.

She gathered up the things she wanted to keep and then headed back to where Travis was just putting the last piece of tape on a box. She deposited the items from the nursery in the last open box and then slid it across the wooden floor to Travis.

"All finished?" he asked with an arched brow.

"Yes. There's still a few things in the garage, and there's a storage shed out back. I can't imagine there's much in either of those locations I'd want to keep." She covered up a yawn and then shook her head, "I'm pretty tired. I didn't sleep much last night."

"I bet you didn't. Let me finish up these two boxes, then we'll head downstairs and you can bed down for the night."

"I can sleep on the couch. The ends recline. Several times, I ended up doing just that when Daniel was sick." Claire said and gave Travis a sad look. "I haven't talked about Scott or Daniel in four years. It kind of feels weird and yet…comforting? Does that make any sense?"

"It makes perfect sense. You've been fighting your memories instead of letting them help you heal. It will get better with each passing day. At least, that's what happened with Emily. My only regret with losing her was the fact that Tyler will never know what an amazing person his mother was."

"Yes, he will, because you'll tell him. You'll show him pictures and talk about her. He'll know." Claire sounded very confident and realized she was also talking to herself.

"We should probably try to get some sleep. Morning is only a few hours away. Is there anything else you want to do before we head back to Chicago?" Travis asked, as they reached the doorway to the living room where Douglas and Tyler were both asleep.

"Can I answer that in the morning?" she hedged. She was exhausted from the day and felt as if there was something she needed to do, but her tired brain was spinning in a million different directions.

"Sure thing." Travis led her over to the unoccupied couch.

When he started to turn away, she threw her arms around him, hugging him from the back. "Thank you for today. Words will never be able to express how much your support meant to me."

Travis extricated himself from her arms and turned to fully face her. He pulled her back into his arms and then tipped her chin up and met her eyes. "I'm glad you brought me along. I don't like thinking that you could have been going through this all alone." He smoothed her hair back and one corner of his mouth quirked upward. "You've gotten beneath my skin, Claire. I know you've got a lot on your plate right now, and I should probably be shot for even going down this road right now, but I'm going to do it anyway. I want you to know that, when the smoke clears from today's revelations, I'm going to be right here waiting for you on the other side."

He brushed a thumb over her lips and then smiled more at her. "You are an amazing woman. I am looking forward to getting to know you a lot better." He paused and then asked, "Are you getting what I'm not saying very well?"

Claire nodded. "I think so."

"Well, just so there's no misunderstandings," he murmured, as he dropped his head and placed a chaste kiss upon her lips. When he drew away, he had a satisfied look in his eyes and was wearing a smile. "I kind of like you. I'm hoping that maybe you might like me back, just a little. We've both loved and lost. I know the way I'm feeling right now isn't something I was looking for. When I lost Emily, I figured I'd never find that kind of relationship with another woman again. Then I met you and something inside of me started to stir."

"When we first met, you scared me," Claire confided in him. "Suddenly, after not allowing myself to feel anything for four long years, I was feeling again. I guess I knew deep down that in order to have the good feelings, I would also have to deal with the bad ones. I tried to run away from them; from how it felt when I looked at you. I didn't want to open myself up to getting my heart broken again, so I tried to convince myself I didn't have one."

"Doesn't work," Travis concurred.

"No, it doesn't. And while today has been an ordeal, I surprisingly feel like there's a light at the end." She took a deep breath and then shook her head, "I'm not making much sense, but before meeting you and Tyler, I was living life inside of a dark hole where I intentionally kept any light from entering. Light meant having to face the past and the pain. I just locked it all away.

"Then you came along, and without meaning to, you obliterated the hole and the light came rushing in so fast, it was hard to process. After today, the hole no longer exists. All of the pain and feelings I ignored are mingling with the light, I guess. I'm rambling, but I think I just need time to get everything kind of figured out."

"I understand. Like I said, I'll be here waiting for you. Whatever you need, a shoulder to cry on, muscles to help move things, someone to listen…if I can help, I will. It sounds crazy, but you matter to me."

"Gee," Claire said, trying to lighten the mood, as it was becoming heavy. "And I don't even know your favorite color."

"Kelly green," Travis fired back immediately.

Claire huffed a small laugh, covering her mouth when Tyler stirred across the room. "Mine's baby blue."

Travis nodded, "Get some sleep, and we'll continue this in"—he glanced at his wristwatch—"approximately five hours."

Smiling, Claire watched him move to the other couch and started unfolding a blanket. She did the same. The moment she settled into the reclining side of the couch, she closed her eyes and sleep claimed her. She couldn't say that today had been a good day, not in the sense that she'd accomplished a lot of things or been victorious in anything. Yet, today had opened the door on the past, and she'd survived. She'd done better than survive, she'd come through it and had dealt with the pain along the way. She'd even made a few decisions about the future. That had to count as a good day in some respect. Tomorrow, hopefully, would be better.

Chapter 14

Claire was walking in the clouds. She didn't know why she was surrounded by the white wisps; but she didn't feel afraid. She felt light, almost as if she was floating along. A bright light, to which she was being drawn, was up ahead. The clouds started to thin out, revealing a beautiful mountain valley. Green grass was dotted with wildflowers in every color imaginable. A brilliant blue sky hung overhead. While she couldn't see the sun, she could feel its warmth.

As she continued to move toward the ground, more details came into view. A large picnic basket and a red-and-white checkered blanket had been arranged on the top of the hill overlooking a placid lake below. Children's laughter reached her ears and she turned to see a man swinging a little girl into the air by her arms. She couldn't see the man's features, but the little girl had curly blonde hair, bright blue eyes, and was looking down on the man with love shining from her eyes.

An older boy ran to join them. His sandy blonde hair was tousled from the slight breeze. He called out to them, and Claire couldn't believe her ears or her eyes. When the young boy turned toward her, she knew she was looking at Daniel. Not her little man who had been hooked up to tubes and machines the last time she saw him, but a vibrant young man full of life and...

If that was Daniel, then the man would have to be...he turned toward her, and Claire felt tears wetting her cheeks. Scott. It was Scott. He looked so good and complete.

She watched, as he pulled the little girl back into his arms and settled her on his hip. He reached for the little boy's hand, and together, they approached the picnic. Claire was stationed on the other side. She watched as they drew nearer. Her eyes were fixated on the little girl who looked like she was around three or four years old. Claire had never seen her before.

Where am I? What is this? Am I...

"You're dreaming," a soft male voice spoke into her mind.

"Dreaming? But Daniel's not a little boy any longer?" she asked the voice in her head.

"No. It's been four years. He's happy in Heaven with his daddy and sister."

"Sister? So, the little girl...she's the baby I lost?"

"Yes. Scott and Daniel were waiting for her. They've been together every day since she arrived."

"I never told Scott..."

"He understood. You also never named her. Scott did that."

"Scott named her?"

"Rachel. It means 'little lamb'. They are waiting for you to finish your work on Earth."

"I'm done. I want to be with them."

"It's not your time, though," the voice told her. "You still have things to accomplish down there and lives to impact. They will always be here for you. Make them proud."

Claire stared at her family until she felt herself pulled way, farther and farther. She couldn't see their faces any longer. "Please. I don't want to leave."

"It's time. Be at peace about the past. Look to the future and make every moment count."

Claire was soon surrounded by the clouds again and then

everything faded away to nothingness.

She awakened with her face awash in tears, and she struggled to process what woke her up. *The dream!*

"Lady, are you okay?" a small voice asked beside the couch.

Tyler stood in his fireman pajamas and a blanket wrapped around his body.

"Hey, Tyler. Shouldn't you still be asleep?"

"You were crying." He climbed up onto the couch, intent on joining her. She scooted over and pulled him up, turning him so that he was sitting between her and the arm of the recliner. "I'm sorry you're sad."

"It's okay. I had a dream."

"A bad dream?" Tyler asked.

Claire thought about that for a moment, and then shook her head. "No, sweetheart. It was a good dream. A wonderful dream, actually, but it made me a little sad. Why don't we both go back to sleep for a bit?"

When he nodded and then snuggled into her side, she wrapped an arm around his shoulders and went back to sleep. Images from her dream filling her with a sense of peace like she hadn't known in years. Everything was going to be alright.

***

Guardian Angel School

Hope watched Matthias, as he entered the schoolroom. She had to resist the urge to go hug her mentor. Angels didn't usually engage in such displays of affection, but she wondered if Matthias would make an exception this once.

"Don't even think about it, Hope. Hugging is not allowed, and you know it."

Hope hid her smile and nodded her head dutifully. "Yes, sir. I just wanted to thank you. Letting Claire see her family in a dream was exactly what she needed. She now knows that Scott and Daniel are happy, and she got to see the baby she lost."

Hope looked up and blinked before informing Matthias, "It's a good thing angels can't cry because I think I'd be what the humans call a watering pot right now."

Matthias chuckled, "Angels don't cry, but it is good that you can empathize with your charge and that you understand how much comfort she will get from tonight's dream."

"Was her husband disappointed that he couldn't communicate with her?" Hope asked. Communication between the physical realm and the heavenly wasn't as unusual as most humans believed. It almost never included conversations between the two souls.

"He understood and was more than grateful for the opportunity to set her mind at ease. He insisted I talk to her and tell her their daughter's name."

"Rachel. I like that," Hope smiled.

"As do I. It was a slight stretch of what I felt comfortable doing, but I could feel the self-imposed guilt leave Claire's mind, as she exited the dream. You should be happy that your plan worked so well."

"I couldn't have done it without you," Hope told him, raising a brow at his attempt to hide a smirk. "Or could I have? Could I have contacted her husband and given Claire a chance to see him and their children in a dream?"

"One day, little angel. You're not quite ready for that level of responsibility, but you are well on your way. I also wanted to congratulate you for taking time to help Joy. You and Charity are doing very well this year, and she needed your encouragement just then."

"I'm glad I could help. Speaking of which, I should probably go see how Claire is going to handle things when she wakes up. There's only six more days until Christmas and she's not even given a thought to the calendar. I'm thinking Tyler could help with that side of things."

"Just don't mess with any human emotions and don't build up false hope where it isn't needed," Matthias warned her.

"I won't. Angel honor." She linked her thumbs and forefingers together in an infinity symbol and smiled at him. "See you later and thanks again."

She started to head back to Earth, but she remembered there was a special choir practice happening. She couldn't think of a better way to celebrate than singing. She did a quick check and saw that Claire was still sleeping and then headed for the choir room. She'd catch up with her charges a little later.

Chapter 15

The next morning…

Claire woke up when Tyler crawled off the chair. She rubbed her eyes and gave him a sleepy smile when he announced to the entire room of still sleeping adults that he was ready for breakfast. Douglas sat up, looked around to get his bearings and grinned at Tyler. "Hey, little man. How's about you and I go rustle up some breakfast for everyone?"

"Pancakes," Tyler announced.

"And we now know what we're eating, just not where. Any suggestions you want to throw out there, Claire?"

"The diner's the only thing in town open this early," Claire answered. She looked at Tyler and told him, "Ask Carl to make you a mouse pancake. They're his specialty."

"Mouse pancakes?" Tyler scrunched up his face. "I don't want to eat a mouse. I want to eat a pancake with lots of syrup."

Claire chuckled, "I promise there are no mice in the pancakes. He just makes them look like the face of a mouse."

"Tyler, why don't you go to the bathroom and brush your teeth, and I'll bring you some clothes to change into?" Travis asked, having woken up and joined the conversation. Once his son had left the living room, he looked at Claire and asked, "Are you okay?"

"I'm fine," she replied, pushing the recliner back into a sitting position and folding up the blanket she'd used.

Douglas left the room. She busied herself straightening the couches and folding up blankets and sheets. Travis mirrored her actions, straightening up the other side of the room. Claire found

132

herself without anything else to do. She looked at Travis, and the idea that had begun to form in her mind would no longer be silenced.

"I need to run a few errands before we head back to Chicago," she told him softly.

"I figured you might. Want some company?"

"Maybe. I need to pay a visit to Marie, and then to the cemetery."

"Does it matter which errand you do first?" Travis asked.

"Kind of," Claire told him quietly. "I need to go see Marie. I'm hoping she can tell me where Scott and Daniel's graves are. I was only there once...for the funeral..."

"And you weren't functioning at your best that day," Travis finished her statement. "I get it. I really do."

Claire nodded and stood up a bit taller. "Would you mind if we just met Douglas and Tyler at the diner?"

"No. Let me go make sure he has everything under control with Tyler, and I'll be ready to go in about fifteen minutes. I could really use a quick shower."

"I was thinking the same thing. I'll use the guest bathroom down here, and you can use one of the showers upstairs."

Travis nodded and gathered up Tyler's clothing along with his own overnight bag. "I'll be as quick as I can."

Claire nodded and headed for the kitchen. She stopped by the stack of boxes in the dining room and located a change of clothing. The guest bathroom was located between the kitchen and the garage. She made short work of rinsing off and getting dressed again. She'd foregone washing her hair. She didn't want to have to wait for it to dry before leaving the house.

A glance outside showed it was currently snowing. Given the grey sky, it didn't plan on stopping anytime soon. She'd decided in that moment that going to the cemetery with wet hair in the middle of December was just asking to get really sick. A complication she didn't need right now in her life.

She heard Travis come down the stairs. She turned and watched him as he finished tidying up things and then joined her. "Everything okay?"

"Fine. Douglas and Tyler are heading for the diner. I told them we would join them as soon as we could. Are you ready to go?"

"I am, but I have to confess, I don't have Marie's address."

"We'll get it from someone, then. Grab your coat and let's head out," Travis suggested, grabbing his own coat and sliding his arms into the sleeves. Claire followed suit before they hurried outside and climbing into his vehicle.

"I will not miss winter when Spring arrives," Travis told her, turning on the ignition and then adjusting the heater dials.

"I agree with you there."

"So, who would be the most likely person to tell us where to find Marie?"

"Marjorie would know, but if we go to the diner, I'm afraid we'll get stuck there."

"Just call her."

Claire nodded and pulled out her cell phone. She knew the diner's number by heart, even though it had been four years since she'd had to use it. *I guess somethings you never forget.*

"Diner," Marjorie's voice came across the line.

"Hey, Marjorie. It's Claire…"

"Oh, girl. How are you doing this morning? Carl and I were just saying one of us should go over and check on you."

"I'm doing okay. Travis's son and his friend are heading your way in a few for some breakfast. I might have mentioned to Tyler something about mouse pancakes," Claire warned her.

Marjorie chuckled, "Noted. Mouse pancakes for the little one. Will you and Travis be joining them?"

"In a bit. I was hoping you could tell me where to find Marie. I wanted to see her…"

"Well, she and her husband have a small house over on Elm Street. The third house on the left side of the street. A little yellow clapboard with a fenced yard."

"I think I can find that. Thank you."

"No problem, child. Give those babies a hug and kiss for me."

Claire smiled, "I'll do that." She disconnected the call and then sighed. "Marie lives a few blocks from here. Go to the end of the street and then turn left."

She watched out the window as they drove, "Not much seems to have changed." She pointed to Elm Street, "Turn there."

Travis came to a stop at the little yellow house. Claire sat, watching it for a long moment and gathering her courage. She owed Marie a debt of gratitude, but words seemed so inadequate.

"Want me to come up with you?" Travis quietly inquired.

"Would you?" Claire asked with a grateful smile.

135

"Of course." Travis turned off and then exited the car, then went around and opening her door when she continued to sit there. "The best way to deal with nerves is to just get it over with."

"Right," Claire told him, stepping out and into the cold. "Brrr. The freezing temperatures are a good motivator. Maybe I should have called first?"

"She has three babies, right? I'm sure she's home," Travis told her.

Claire led the way to the front door and depressed the doorbell before shoving her hands in her pockets. A moment later, the front door opened and a face she recognized looked back at her. Shock filling the other woman's eyes.

"Hi."

"Claire? Oh, my god. Come inside, please. What are you doing here?" Marie grabbed her hand and pulled her inside with Travis following, then he shut the door.

Marie looked at her and then pulled her into a warm hug. "You look good."

Claire hugged her back, realizing how much she'd missed human contact in her self-imposed prison. "You look good, too. I heard you got married and had triplets?"

Marie released her and giggled. "Triplets. Who would have thought? I mean, the idea was intriguing, but the reality is exhausting." Just then a cry echoed from the small white box attached to her waist. "Speak of the little devils. Follow me, and you'll get a firsthand look at my life now. Chasing bad guys and speeders was nothing compared to motherhood."

Claire remembered the chaos of having a single child. As she followed Marie through a living room filled with small bouncy seats and piles of laundry, she wondered how Marie wasn't going a bit crazy. The kitchen was no better, filled with three highchairs and the kitchen table had been pushed into a corner. Only two chairs were visible. A small Christmas tree sat in the middle of the table, just a few decorations adorning its boughs.

They turned down the hallway next to a small closet that clearly held the washer and dryer, both currently in operation and piled high with additional loads. There were two bedrooms, one held two cribs and a changing table, the other held a full-sized bed and another crib. Claire watched as Marie picked up the crying infant and expertly changed his diaper, then placed him in a dry sleeper.

"Hey, Charlie. I want you to meet someone very special. This is Claire." Marie looked behind her and then raised a brow, "And you are?"

"Travis. A friend from Chicago."

Marie nodded at him and then looked down at her son, "Charlie, meet Travis."

A cry from the other bedroom came, followed quickly by a third. "Guess naptime is over." Marie looked at Claire, "Would you mind holding him for a few minutes?"

Claire shook her head and took the little boy into her arms, watching him as he looked at her with wide brown eyes. "Hey, there Charlie. Aren't you a good boy?"

Marie slipped past them and into the other bedroom and Claire could hear her talking to Victoria and Alexander. She looked at Travis and then nodded toward the hallway. "Why don't we go back into the living room?"

"Sure," Travis led the way and, after moving some clothes baskets, Claire and he both sat down. Claire held Charlie, who had decided to suck his thumb and lay his head on her shoulder while

137

she rubbed his back. Claire looked around the small house and wondered how Marie and her husband were going to handle living in such a small place when the children got a little bigger. In not even a year, they would all three be moving around like human tornadoes and this house was simply too small for five people.

Marie joined them, a child on each hip. Claire took a good look at her. She was tired, wearing a dirty t-shirt, and her hair looked greasy as if she hadn't had a chance to wash it in several days. She sank down on a chair and gave Claire a forced smile.

"Sorry about that. Naptime usually lasts a bit longer. They'll be hungry soon."

"Marie, I don't mean to pry, but why are you and Tim living in such a small place?"

Marie shook her head, "We bought this place before I got pregnant. It would have been fine for a single baby, but with three...well, it's crowded. We thought we might have time to sell this one and look for something better, but the babies came early."

Claire nodded her head, "Having a new baby in the house is a life-changer. I remember those first few months. Frankly, I couldn't have handled three at one time."

"I thought having one was hard," Travis interjected. "May I take one of them?" Victoria and Alexander had decided to take turns pulling on Marie's sloppy ponytail.

"You don't mind?" Marie asked dubiously.

"I have a four-year old little boy currently seeking mouse pancakes at the diner," he told her, taking Alexander from her arms.

Marie relaxed a bit and then smiled at Claire. "What have you been doing since you left here?"

"I moved to Chicago, and I'm working. I came back to get

my license."

"So, you're still doing preschool?" Marie asked.

Claire shook her head, "No. Well, Travis is having me help him set up a childcare center for his business, but I haven't really had much to do with children since I left here."

Marie nodded, "I can understand that. I'm glad you came back and came to see me."

"I wanted to say thank you for everything you did for me four years ago."

"No thanks are needed," Marie assured her.

Claire nodded and the idea that had begun to form in her head earlier grew. She suddenly knew it was the right path to take. "Actually, they are and I'm hoping you might consider helping me out."

Chapter 16

Marie nodded, "If I can, I'd be happy to."

"Oh, you can. Let me tell you a story." Claire told her how she'd left the real estate agent and the lawyer in charge of disposing of the house and her belongings. As she talked, Marie smiled and nodded, fully aware that the town had all chipped into keep the house and yard presentable, for what they hoped would be Claire's homecoming one day.

"Anyway, I didn't know any of this until yesterday. To say I was shocked is an understatement. When Marjorie told me about you and Tim, and your three precious babies, an idea began to form."

Claire paused and then met Marie's eyes. "I want you and Tim to move your family into the house."

"What?" Marie asked, her eyebrows disappearing up her forehead.

"It's the perfect house to raise a family in. There are four bedrooms and several bathrooms. It has a big yard, and best of all, it's completely paid for so you and Tim could pay me whatever you could afford. After this house sold."

Marie shook her head, "We could never…"

"Of course, you can. I need you to do this because I'm going back to Chicago, and there's no reason for that house to sit there empty, waiting for a family to live there again. Please, will you at least mention it to Tim?"

A scuffle of feet in the doorway drew everyone's attention to the man standing there, a look of disbelief on his face. Claire smiled at him, "Tim, did you hear what I just told Marie?"

"I did, and…it's such a generous offer, I'm not even sure what to say."

"Say yes and convince your wife that this is a blessing," Claire told him.

Travis stood up and then suggested, "Why don't you and Marie talk things over? We're supposed to meet my son and friend at the diner for breakfast. You can come find us there in an hour?"

Tim nodded and then stepped forward and took Alexander from his arms. "One hour. We'll talk about it."

"Good," Claire told them both, handing him Charlie as well. "Goodbye, sweet babies. Convince your momma and daddy to let you all move."

Claire followed Travis out to the car and was silent as he drove them back toward the center of town. When they reached Main Street, she turned and asked, "Are you shocked?"

"That you made such a generous offer?" When she nodded, he shook his head, "Not at all. I think it's actually a perfect solution. You will get joy from knowing Marie and her family are living in that house. You won't have to wait for it to sell, it's a tangible way for you to express your thanks for her support."

"That's exactly why I made the offer. I don't need that house, nor could I ever come back here and live in it. There are just too many memories. I realized that this morning, but the house was built for a family, and I can't think of anyone I'd rather see living there than Marie and Tim."

"Let's hope they see it that way, as well." They arrived at the diner, and he parked in front. "Let me come get your door. It's pretty icy out there."

Claire nodded and waited for him to open her door. She took his offered hand, but just as she put her weight on her feet, they started to slip. Suddenly, her nose was buried in his chest, and his arms were wrapped tightly around her.

"Whoa! I've got you," Travis murmured against her ear.

Claire clung to his hand and his shoulder, inhaling his clean scent and biting her lip as her body betrayed her. She'd told herself she wasn't interested in any sort of romantic relationship, but her mind and her senses didn't seem to be on the same page at all. Her heart skipped a beat when he reached up and tipped her head back so that he could see her eyes.

"Are you okay?"

She nodded, unable to speak and finally found the strength to push away from him and stand on her own.

"You were right, it is a bit slippery out here. Let's go eat," she told him brightly, hoping she'd adequately covered up the effects of being in his arms. Her cheeks were flushed, which could easily be blamed on the cold wind, but not her racing heart. That was all because of Travis.

He nodded but kept hold of her hand. When she tried to retrieve it, he pulled it even closer and shook his head. "I like you right where you are."

A thrill shot through her. She smiled softly and looked down. *I like it too.*

Douglas and Tyler were already seated, and just as she'd promised, Tyler was doing his best to consume a giant mouse pancake.

"Claire! They do have mouse pancakes," he exclaimed, as they slid into the booth across from him.

"I told you so," she replied.

Marjorie appeared with two menus and a smile, "Did you find Marie's house?"

"I did. I also offered to let her, and Tim move into the house."

Marjorie's smile broadened, "Bless you for thinking of that. She and that little family of hers do not fit in that tiny house." Marjorie's smile fell as she asked, "Did she accept?"

"Tim came home as I was making the offer, so they are discussing it. They're supposed to meet us here with an answer in a little while."

"Well, if that girl lets pride keep her from accepting a Christmas miracle like the one you just offered her, I'll personally take her in the back room and give her a talking to."

Claire smiled at the image and nodded, "I'll let you know if I need your help."

"Good. So, what are you two eating for breakfast?"

Travis glanced at the menu and then smiled, "Surprise me. I like a little bit of everything."

"Oh, honey. You don't know what you just invited." Marjorie turned and hollered toward the kitchen window, "Carl, fix us up a diner special."

"On it," Carl's voice echoed back.

Travis leaned over and whispered to Claire, "What is a diner special?"

Claire smiled, "You're about to find out. Don't worry if you can't eat it all. No one will be offended, I promise." She closed her menu and then gave Marjorie her order for a small omelet and toast.

"Be right back. Tyler, how is that mouse doing?"

Tyler grinned, syrup on either side of his mouth, "Gooood."

"Great."

"This little town seems like a nice place to have grown up," Douglas commented.

Claire shrugged, "I guess it was. It still is for many people."

"Just not you?" he queried.

"Not anymore. Too many memories, but this morning they don't seem quite so hard to bear."

"It will get easier with time," Travis agreed. "So, assuming Marie and her husband are going to move into the house, that means we have our work cut out for us to get everything else packed up and loaded into the moving truck."

"It won't take long, unless you've changed your mind about the furniture?" Douglas asked.

"No, I haven't. I want Marie and Tim to use it, if they want. If not, they can sell it and use the money to buy something they can use."

"That sounds a lot like someone playing Santa Claus," a male voice said from behind them.

Chapter 17

Claire turned and then smiled as she recognized Jim Akens and his wife. "Hello."

"Hello, back. I heard you were in town and was hoping I'd have a chance to see for myself that you were doing okay."

Claire smiled, "I'm doing fine." She introduced everyone and then asked, "You're still with the force?"

"Till I retire," he agreed. "I overheard you telling Marjorie the offer you made to Marie. I'll second my support to getting that stubborn couple to accept. Everyone's been a bit concerned about them raising those three babies in that tiny space."

"It solves a huge problem for me and seems like a great solution for them at the same time. It's not charity. I expect them to make me a solid offer for it, not because I need the money, but because they need to do that to salvage their pride."

"Smart woman. I always knew that. You're doing the right thing, and I'm sure they'll see that, if they can think straight as exhausted as they are. Anyway, I just wanted to say hi and tell you I'm off and wouldn't mind helping you load whatever stuff you're taking back to Chicago with you."

"That would be appreciated," Travis nodded.

"Yes, it would," Claire told him.

"Good. We'll meet you over at the house in an hour or so." Jim and his wife stood up after dropping some bills on the table. As they were preparing to leave, he turned and squatted down so that he was speaking directly to Claire. "Have you been to the cemetery yet?"

Claire swallowed and shook her head, her expression darkening as bad memories began to surface. "No."

"You should. Closure and all that."

Claire nodded and, when he stood up, she reached out and stopped him. "Um…if I did decide to go there, where…"

"Is the grave?" Jim asked. She nodded, and he smiled softly. "Next to the guardian angel statue in the central garden."

Claire felt tears fill her eyes as she nodded again. "Thanks."

Travis stood up and walked a few steps with Jim. The two men spoke softly for a moment before Travis returned as did Marjorie with their food. He waited until she'd served them before he leaned over and whispered, "Do you want to go there after breakfast?"

She nodded, not even trying to put what she was feeling into words. Travis reached for her hand and squeezed it tightly before releasing it to dig into every breakfast food imaginable, topped off with a delicious-looking country fried steak covered in pepper gravy.

"This looks amazing, but enough food to feed a small army."

"No one has ever finished it all without getting a tummy ache," she warned him. "Don't feel like you have to eat it all. We have a long drive ahead of us."

"Noted. Douglas. Tyler. Help yourselves."

Claire glanced at Tyler who was staring at his father's plate with wide eyes. "Your son seems to be in shock."

Douglas chuckled, closing Tyler's bottom jaw with his finger. "Finish your mouse pancake, then you and I have a date with the snow in Claire's backyard."

"What?" she asked.

"Tyler has requested we play in the snow before driving home. Since I was wise enough to grab his snow suit, I agreed."

"Good, that will keep him occupied while Claire and I make one more stop." Travis turned his attention back to his food, as did everyone else.

Claire finished her meal, then watched Travis as he attempted to do justice to Carl's cooking. He finally gave up and pushed his plate away with a groan. "If I eat one more bite, I'm going to need a hospital."

Claire grinned, nodding in response to the wink Marjorie sent her as she cleaned up the table behind them. "Want me to ask for a box?"

Travis looked horrified, "Since I'm never eating again, in a word…No."

Marjorie smiled. "I heard that."

"Sorry," Travis told her. "Tell your husband he's a very good cook, but I don't eat like I did when I was eighteen. Not unless I want to buy a new wardrobe every week."

Claire glanced at him and shook her head. "Don't tell me you're one of those health nuts?"

"Not, just that when I turned twenty-five, I noticed my waistline expanding and my pants were staying the same. I try to do a few miles on a treadmill several times a week, but honestly, I'd rather be outside hiking or enjoying nature than working out."

The bell over the front door jingled and Marjorie smiled, "Tim and Marie are here. I'll go grab a baby and find some others to hold the other two. Send up a smoke signal if you need backup."

Claire turned and watched as Marjorie immediately absconded with an infant. Within moments, two other customers came forward and took possession of the other infants.

Tim and Marie joined them. Douglas took his clue to hustle Tyler back into his coat. "Time to go play in the snow."

Carl appeared from the back and quickly cleared the table, merely shaking his head at Travis when he saw the food still left on the platter. "City boys."

Travis rolled his eyes good naturedly, then greeted Tim and Marie. "Have a seat."

"Thank you." Tim held out a chair for his wife and then seated himself.

Claire smiled at the gentlemanly gesture, pleased that Marie had married someone who knew how to treat a lady. "Did you have a chance to discuss my offer?"

Tim and Marie shared a look and then said, "We did. We would be pleased to take you up on your kind offer, but we are going to pay you for the house. We'll need to sell ours and then get another loan…"

"No need to get a loan for the house. I'll be happy to carry the note for you. There's no hurry on my end, so feel free to move in anytime, even today if you want. Once you've sold the other house, we'll draw up some sort of sale agreement."

"That's so generous…"

"It's something I'm glad I can do."

Marie had tears in her eyes and reached across the table and took Claire's hands. "You can't know how much this is going to bless us. You're like our own personal St. Nicholas."

Claire held her smile in place and shook her head. "No, just repaying a debt and helping us both out in the process. By the way, you have some loyal friends here. Both Marjorie and Tim promised to have a stern talk with you if you didn't accept my offer."

Marie smiled and then wiped away her tears. "This town is pretty special."

"I'm remembering that. Who knows, maybe I'll come back from time to time," Claire murmured, finding the idea less than repugnant, which in itself was surprising.

Tim and Marie stayed a few more minutes and promised to meet them at the house a few hours from now. It wouldn't take them very long to load the moving truck, and Claire wanted to give them a chance to look over the house and ask any questions they might have. When and how they moved in would be up to them. Since half the town would know within the hour what had just transpired, she knew they would have more than enough help over the coming days.

"That's a pretty special thing you just did," Travis told her, as they left the diner and got back into the vehicle. "You're a pretty special woman."

Claire fastened her seatbelt, unsure of how to receive his praise. She was actually serving herself by getting rid of the house. While she admitted she was helping out someone who had once selflessly helped her, she was more focused on the fact that she no longer had to worry about a house that she hadn't even realized she still owned. "I did what anyone would have done in the circumstances."

"Hardly, but we can debate that later. I saw the cemetery when we drove into town. Is that where I'm going?"

Claire nodded, a knot forming in her stomach, as Travis started the car and headed toward the edge of town. This would be a defining moment and while hard, it was also something she was certain she needed to do. After the dream…well, she needed to share that with someone, but she wanted a chance to talk to Scott one last time before she shared it with anyone.

Rachel. That's what Scott named our daughter.

Claire stared out the window, as the cemetery came into view. There were several tall statues in the garden, but the one with his wings extended over the grave sites nearby had always been one of her favorites. She'd forgotten that Scott and Daniel had been buried there. Now, she took a measure of comfort in knowing that an angel watched over them.

Chapter 18

Hope had already gone to the cemetery, pleased to see that someone had shoveled the walkways and the elegant marble headstone that marked the final resting place of Claire's loved ones was very easy to find. She settled on the shoulders of the angel statue, looking at the face and wondering how a human had gotten Michelangelo's countenance so accurately. The straight Aquiline nose, high cheekbones, and passive expression were exactly what anyone would see if they were to encounter the Archangel.

"Seems like maybe angels have been using dreams to communicate more often than I realized," she murmured to herself, as she watched Travis and Claire get out of the vehicle.

She watched them approach the statue, with Travis stopping fifty feet away and speaking softly to Claire.

"I'll wait here and give you some privacy," he told her, tugging her winter hat a bit lower over her ears.

Claire nodded and then turned and slowly approached the headstone. Snow had piled up along the bottom half. Claire immediately bent down and started wiping the snow away with her gloved hands. Hope watched her, knowing the minute she saw the inscription and the drawing that had been inscribed on the bottom.

Claire sat back on her heels, covering her mouth with a gloved hand as tears streamed down her face. The headstone had been inscribed after the funeral, but Claire had never come to visit it; not once before she'd fled the pain and heartbreak that lie in Winchester.

Here lies Scott St. Peters,

Beloved husband and Loving father.

He will forever hold in his arms his son,

Daniel James,

And the infant he never got to meet while on Earth,

His precious lamb.

May God hold them forever in His hands

Until one day, we meet again.

Claire sobbed openly now, removing her gloves and tracing the inscribed letters on the headstone. "Scott, I don't know if you can hear me, but I miss you so much. I'm sorry I didn't honor our love by grieving you these last four years. It just hurt so much to think about all I'd lost, and to think that I'd lost the last piece of you…it was almost too much to bear.

"I saw you last night. With Daniel and…Rachel. Thank you for naming her. I don't know how I saw you last night, but I know it was you and that you were sending me a message. I miss you so much, but it helps to know that Daniel and our daughter are with you. I so wish I could have seen her or held her, just once before she was taken away from me.

"And Daniel, I hope you didn't suffer those last few days, sweetheart. Your little body was so damaged. The doctors did everything they could, but it wasn't enough."

She stopped talking and just let her tears flow, a catharsis that was long overdue. When her fingers were numb with cold, she realized she was shivering uncontrollably. She'd been sitting there for an unknown length of time and needed to move. She flexed her fingers, struggling to pull her gloves back on, but she was too cold

Suddenly, Travis was there, kneeling in the snow next to her. He carefully pulled her gloves on and then lifted her to her feet. He steadied her when her frozen knees refused to cooperate and held onto her until she was finally able to stand on her own.

Hope watched the couple, trying to figure out how best to help them. She thought about sending a few thoughts their direction. Right now, Claire was so emotionally fragile. Sent thoughts could easily be seen by Hope's superiors as a violation of the guardian angel code. They weren't allowed to influence human emotions, especially when it came to how they felt about a fellow human.

Suddenly, Matthias was hovering near her. "Little angel, how goes it with your charges?"

Hope took a moment and put on a bright smile. "Very good."

Matthias glanced down at the couple and then arched a brow at her. "Really? It appears as if Claire has been crying."

"She just finished visiting the gravesite of her husband and son. She also read the inscription, and it confirmed in her mind that the dream last night wasn't just her imagination. It was a message from above."

Matthias dropped down and read the inscription. He nodded and then returned to her side. "It seems your idea of having her late husband communicate with her was right on the mark. So, what are your plans now? There are only six days left."

"I know. I'm still working on that," Hope told him, her attention going back to the couple below. She really didn't know how she was going to get Claire to like Christmas again. Travis was already on the way to falling in love with Claire, but the woman was fighting her attraction to him.

Come on, Claire. Take a chance on love again.

153

***

"Are you ready to leave?" Travis asked, as Claire began walking back toward the vehicle.

"I am. Marie should be at the house and, as soon as we've loaded up and I've handed back the keys, I'd like to head home. I need to be back in Chicago, so that I can process everything."

Travis nodded and took her hand, steadying her as she sank into the leather seat and buckled up. He drove them straight to the house. Within twenty minutes of their arrival, the last box of Claire's past life was loaded into the moving truck.

Tyler had been helping them, but now he was fading, as Douglas and Travis consulted on their return to Chicago. After a brief conversation, Travis kissed Tyler goodbye and watched as Douglas led him to the moving truck and secured him in the child seat.

"We'll take the truck back to the parking garage, and I'll make sure this little man gets some dinner before he heads off to bed."

"We'll be right behind you, maybe an hour at the most," Travis told him.

"No problem. Drive safely. There's another storm supposed to be moving in tonight."

"You as well. Tyler, you have fun with Douglas. I'll see you tonight before you go to bed."

Tyler lurched at Travis, giving him a big hug before placing a smacking kiss on his cheek. "Bye, daddy."

"Bye, squirt."

Tyler squirmed to get down, but once his feet were on the

floor, he headed for Claire instead of Douglas. He lifted his arms, and she instinctively picked him up.

"Lady Claire?"

"Yes, Tyler?"

He placed a hand on both of her cheeks and searched her eyes, then whispered, "You're pretty. I like it better when you smile."

"I like it better when I smile, too," she told him back. "I'll try to do it more from now on."

"Good." Tyler kissed her on the nose and then wiggled to get down. He ran back to Douglas. Claire and Travis watched as they headed out to the big moving truck.

"Well, that was fun," Travis told her drolly.

She chuckled and then waved as Tim and Marie came around the corner of the street, driving a family van. "They're here."

She waited on the front step until they reached her. Then she ushered them into their new home to give them a brief tour which ended in the kitchen.

"As you can see, I've left the furniture and many other items. If you can use them, please consider them yours. If you decide to decorate or replace them, I hope you'll consider selling them and using the money to help others."

"Of course, but we could always send the money to you…"

"I have no need of it. I've barely spent any of Scott's life insurance," she assured them. "Do you have any other questions?"

"Not right now, but I'm sure we might in the future."

Claire jotted down her cell phone number on the fridge.

155

"Call me if you have any questions at all." She shook Tim's hand and then hugged Marie twice. "I'm so happy for you."

Marie hugged her back with tears in her eyes, "You don't know what you've done."

"Yes, I do." Claire released her and then grabbed her coat and headed for the front door where Travis was already waiting. Tim and Marie followed her; their arms wrapped around one another.

Claire turned back before she closed the car door and waved.

"Merry Christmas," Marie called out.

Claire opened her mouth, but she couldn't get the words out. Instead, she smiled and replied, "Happy New Year."

It was many miles down the road before Travis asked her about her inability to acknowledge Christmas. She really didn't have a good excuse now; none that would hold up to scrutiny.

Chapter 19

Two days later…

Claire arrived at work, but ignored Alex calling her name. She skirted around the mobile coffee carton on the sidewalk and, using the patron entrance, entered the department store. It wasn't her favorite way to arrive at her destination, but she didn't have the patience to deal with Alex's flirting today. It was December 21st. The company Christmas party was that evening.

It was also the unveiling of the new childcare center. When Travis had told her that he planned to have it ready in only two days, Claire had laughed in his face. The idea was ludicrous, but she hadn't known that he'd already been setting things in motion before they'd even left Chicago. When they'd arrived at the building the day after their return, she'd been shocked to see how the childcare area had been transformed. Claire had counted no less than fifty workmen in the area, all working to finish the project in record time.

Bright colors were everywhere. She noticed separate rooms with child-sized furniture inside along with cribs, rocking chairs, playsets, and more learning toys and materials than Claire had ever seen in one place at one time.

"What did you do?" she asked.

"I just purchased a few things. I wasn't quite sure what to put where, so I'll need your help sorting everything out before tomorrow night," Travis had told her with a wink.

"You really plan to give the employees tours of this area tomorrow night?"

"What better way to introduce the new benefit to them? Everyone will be enjoying the evening, and this will give them one

157

more thing to celebrate."

Claire had sighed and then spent the next ten hours moving things from one room to another. She and Travis had finally stopped at six o'clock that evening. He'd insisted on having Douglas drive her home. He'd wanted to take her for dinner first, but Claire was dead on her feet and had politely refused.

Now, it was day two, and she was still exhausted. Her dreams had been filled with Scott and Daniel mixed with other images. She hadn't been getting much sleep. She covered up a yawn while riding the escalator to the second floor. She nodded at the clerk behind the customer service window, as she walked through the doors and then stopped to look down at the amazing place Travis had created. Large windows had been placed so that parents could check in on their children during the breaks and lunches without having to disturb them.

All children would be checked in on the second floor. The secured doors to the childcare center were directly adjacent to the employee lounge and locker room. She swiped her security badge and stepped into the reception room, then nodded her approval at the two employees who had been hired to man this station during open hours. She then took the stairs down to the ground floor, her eyes scanning everything as she walked through the various spaces. She nodded at the new employees Travis had hired to help staff the childcare center and pointedly walked past the darkened director's office.

Travis was still convinced that she was perfectly situated to handle that position. He kept bringing it up, obviously deciding to nag her until she finally agreed. Since returning from Winchester, Claire had to admit that the idea of working around children again held an allure she was finding hard to ignore. She just wasn't sure she was entirely ready to take on the responsibility he was offering her. She walked through the third classroom and finally found

158

Travis and Tyler in the playroom.

Travis had insisted that children needed a safe place to play, regardless of the fact that they were inside a building. Synthetic turf had been laid down and the walls had been painted a light blue with clouds and bright lights that simulated sunshine overhead. Small playground equipment, including a slide, monkey bars, and swings had also been added. It was like an indoor park and like nothing Claire had ever seen. The former warehouse space had afforded them the high ceilings needed to carry out such an area, and since it was already equipped with the most modern fire suppression system, that had sped things along considerably.

"I can't believe this place," she told him, as she watched Tyler climb up the stairs and go down the slide.

"I told you I didn't believe in doing anything halfway. In places where the weather is conducive to an outdoor space, we'll try to have an indoor and an outdoor area for children to play." Travis's phone buzzed, and he looked at the message before smiling. "The state inspector is on his way here to give us the final stamp of approval."

"What? I thought he wasn't going to come until next week. After Christmas?"

"I convinced him to move the calendar up since this was such a unique facility. He was anxious to see it after I described some of the features and was more than happy to postpone his holiday for half a day to come by and visit us."

Claire looked at Travis while whispering to him, "We won't pass. We can't."

"Why not? We've crossed our T's and dotted our I's. You said so yourself."

"Most of them. In order to pass, you must have a licensed

159

director on staff."

"Ah! I thought I had already offered the position to a qualified individual."

"I told you…"

"I asked you to give it a shot. A fair trial." Travis stepped closer to her and cupped her cheek. "You said you would try, but this sounds like giving up. What are you so afraid of?"

Claire searched his eyes, then sighed. "I'm afraid I might like it too much."

"Does the idea of being happy worry you? The fear that you might actually find love and happiness down here without Scott and your children?"

Claire nodded. "How did you know?"

"Because I have the same fear; although, since meeting you, I'm finding the future much more promising."

She looked down, then she took his hand and pulled him over to one of the park benches on the outskirts of the playground. "I never told you about the dream I had the night we stayed in Winchester."

"No, but I figured something must have happened. You were a lot calmer the next morning."

"I saw Scott. In my dreams. He was with Daniel and the baby I lost. A daughter. He didn't actually talk to me, but I could hear this voice in my head. He named our daughter Rachel. It means little lamb."

She paused and then told him, "When I saw the headstone and read what had been inscribed on it, it was like a confirmation that I wasn't crazy; the dream was significant and meaningful."

"That's amazing. The headstone...its inscription was..."

"I know. Before the dream ended, I was told to live my life to the fullest and to never worry about what was to come next. Scott and our children would be waiting there when it was my time."

Travis remained quiet, so she finally asked, "Don't you have anything to say?"

"Only to ask whether or not you intend to follow the advice?"

"I'm going to try," Claire informed him. "They looked so peaceful and happy...I wanted nothing more than to join them. The voice told me I couldn't. Not yet. I was still needed down here."

"Who do you think was speaking in your mind?" he asked.

"I don't know. I think, if it was God, I would have felt more awe...if that makes any sense. But I just felt a sense of peace."

"Good. That's really good. Now, I'm going to tell you about my experience. After Emily died, I wanted to do the same thing. Just give up and join her in Heaven, but there was this little life waiting and watching my every move. My family knocked some sense into me, but it was watching Tyler experience everything for the first time that really hooked me into the childcare business."

"It's also what helped bring me out of depression. I realized, with some help, that I needed to start living for myself, or I wouldn't be any good for Tyler."

"You were lucky to have someone like that in your life," she murmured.

"Yes. But you also had people in your life to take your focus off the bad things."

"I did, but four years ago I...well, I ran away. I needed some space where I could stop hurting, and I couldn't do that in Winchester. Everywhere I looked was another source of pain."

"So, you came to Chicago?"

"Yes. I thought it would be easier to lose myself in a big city. I didn't realize to what extent I was actually trying to lose myself."

"Mr. Hammerstein, there's a gentleman up at the front asking for you," an employee called out from the doorway to the playground.

"I'll be right there. Go ahead and start leading him back." He called Tyler to him and then looked at Claire, "Ready?"

"Sure, but we still…"

"Give this new position a trial run. Say, until the end of January?" Travis asked, as they walked toward the exit.

"That's too long," she told him.

"Not if you like it," he fired back. "End of January."

"December. I'll know if this is something I can do by then," Claire told him.

"That's only a week and a half away," Travis complained.

"That's all I can commit to right now," she told him.

Travis gave her another look as they entered the connected classrooms and saw the suited man waiting for them. "Let's finish this discussion this evening. I'll pick you up at six."

"What? I'm not going tonight…"

"Yes, you are. Who better to show everyone around this place, but you?"

Claire shook her head. The last place she wanted to be was at a Christmas party. She didn't do Christmas. "I don't think…"

Travis smiled at her and then stepped around her and held out his hand to the newcomer. "Travis Hammerstein."

"Oliver Winston. This is quite the facility you have here."

"Thank you. May I introduce Claire St. Peters, our director?"

"Very nice to meet you, Miss St. Peters. I had a chance to visit the preschool you set up in Winchester six years ago, and I must say that I was impressed to find out that Mr. Hammerstein here had snagged you."

"I'm sorry I don't remember you from before," Claire answered softly.

"Oh, I was a tagalong back then. Anyway, I have your application, and I was hoping you could show me around while I'll ask a few questions."

"Claire would be happy to give you a tour. I'm going to get Tyler settled, and I'll join you in a few minutes."

"Very good, Mr. Hammerstein…"

"Please, call me Travis. Mr. Hammerstein was either my grandfather or my dad. I'm neither."

"I can relate to that. Very well, Travis. I look forward to having you join us soon."

Claire took Mr. Winston through the childcare center, answered his questions to the best of her ability, and played the part of the new director. Travis joined them half an hour after they began. Claire stepped back and let him amaze the man with how quickly everything had come together.

"Mr. Hammerstein…Travis," Mr. Winston corrected himself. "What you've done here is amazing. Simply amazing. You should be very proud of yourself. You too, Miss St. Peters."

"Does that mean you'll give us your stamp of approval?" Travis asked with an easy smile.

"Yes, certainly. I'll have it drawn up this afternoon and mailed out first thing in the morning. You should have it in hand the day after."

"December 23rd. What did I tell you, Claire? I was sure we could get this done before Christmas. The employees can try it out the week after."

"Well," Mr. Winston said, "I will let you both get back to your day. It was a pleasure to visit with you and to see this wonderful place. I'll be telling my superiors about the good work you've done here. You can expect to hear from them after the first of the year. They will want to see this place for themselves."

"We'll look forward to giving them a grand tour," Travis smiled. "Let me see you out."

Chapter 20

Claire watched both men walk toward the exit and finally took a moment to sit down. She was right outside the director's office. After only a moment's debate, she got up and walked inside. It was a very pleasant and peaceful office with both a desk and a sitting area. A bank of video screens on the wall adjacent to the desk gave her an instantaneous view of all areas of the childcare center. What Travis had done here, in just a few days' time, was miraculous.

There's that word again. Miraculous. Miracles.

At one time, Claire had believed in miracles wholeheartedly. She'd stopped four years ago. In the last few days, she'd seen evidence all around her that they still existed. She'd even been part of a few of them, which was also something she was still trying to process.

"Claire! Claire!" Tyler's little voice called out to her.

She stepped out of the office, and he immediately ran to her and threw his arms around her knees. "You get to come with us."

"I do?" She looked up and saw Travis watching them from several feet away. "Where are we going?"

"To get a Christmas tree." Tyler still embraced her knees, as Claire took time to measure her response.

"Oh."

"Yes...oh!" Travis came forward, his eyes never leaving hers. "Come with us. It will help you get into the Christmas spirit for tonight's gala."

"I already told you..."

165

"I'm not taking no for an answer. I already asked Sarah to have some dresses delivered from the floor for you to choose from. They should be in my office now. You can pick your dress, and then we'll play hooky for the remainder of the afternoon."

"I don't play hooky," she informed him with a straight face. In truth, she really didn't. Claire was a diligent worker and believed in putting in a full day's work for a day's pay.

"The boss is ordering you to, so you'd best comply. Tyler, let's go get Claire a dress for tonight's party."

Tyler grabbed both their hands and then pulled his feet up so that they were lifting him off the ground. His giggle was contagious and, by the time the elevator arrived to take them to the top floor, Claire was smiling and giggling right along with him.

The dresses Sarah had chosen were elegant and exactly the type of dresses Claire would have selected for herself. They were also all in her size. She'd tried enough dresses on from these brands that she didn't need to try anything on. She selected an elegant sheath in a shimmery gold-colored fabric, knowing her sling back gold-colored heels would go perfectly with it.

"Find one to your liking?" Travis asked.

"Yes." Claire nodded and then almost gasped when she saw the price tag. She covered up her reaction with a slight cough, but Travis wasn't fooled.

"The company is paying for this, so don't worry about it. Being the director of the new childcare center has its perks. This is one of them."

"Travis, this is…"

He reached out and covered her lips with a long finger. "I believe the words you are looking for are 'thank you for the dress.

I'll be ready on time'."

"Thank you for the dress, and I'll be ready on time," she parroted back.

Travis smiled and raised a brow in disbelief. "You're not going to fight me on it?"

"Is there any chance I might win?" she asked softly.

"No." Travis took a step forward until there were only a few inches between them. Tyler had stayed in the foyer with Sarah, leaving him and Claire all alone for the moment. "There's something about you…"

Claire searched his eyes and then her gaze fell to his mouth. He'd kissed her once before, but it had been almost platonic. She suddenly needed to know what it would feel like if he really kissed her. She leaned toward him, and he needed no further incentive.

He slid a hand beneath her hair, cupping her neck and tipping her head back as his lips descended to hers. He kissed her gently as first, deepening the kiss when her hands came up and wrapped over his shoulders.

Claire moan softly at the feel of his muscles beneath her hands, the smell of his aftershave, and the feel of his lips moving over hers. Even though they were only kissing, her body was on fire.

Her hands wrapped around his neck, and he pulled her fully against his chest, smoothing his hands down her back, but stopping when they reached her waistband. He lifted his head and whispered, "I've been wanting to do that for two days."

"Why didn't you?" she asked, leaning her forehead against his chest, as she tried to convince her heart to slow down.

"I was trying to give you time and space. Are you telling me you don't want or need that from me?"

"I don't know," she whispered into his shirt.

"Did I overstep by kissing you?"

"No," she hurried to tell him, lifting her head and then leaning up on her toes and kissing him briefly to emphasize her words. "No. I wanted you to kiss me."

"But this is all confusing, isn't it?" Travis guessed.

"Yeah." *Really confusing. Part of me wants you to kiss me again, and the other part of me feels as if I've just committed a crime against my dead husband.*

"I have a suggestion," Travis told her. He stepped away and took her hand. "Spend Christmas with Tyler and me. My family all gathers at my grandmother's estate for Christmas dinner, but after tonight, I was planning to take a few days off and just enjoy the season with my son. Spend it with me. The center won't open until after we return December 26th. Spend the next few days with us and let's explore this thing building between us."

"I don't celebrate Christmas…"

"Correction. You used to celebrate Christmas and then stopped for a while to grieve. It's time for you to start living again, in all areas. Starting now. Can you honestly tell me you want to spend Christmas alone this year?"

Claire looked at him and, after a moment, she shook her head. "Last year I didn't even think about it. This year…it's different. I really don't want to be alone."

"Then spend it with us. We can start right now. We'll go pick out a tree and then stop by your place and you can pack a bag and some clothes."

"I can stay at my apartment…"

"I'd rather have you with us. It will save a lot of driving back and forth and give us more time to spend together once Tyler goes down for the night."

Claire hesitated. She wanted to accept what he was offering her so badly, but there was still that little bit of guilt that she was living her life while Scott couldn't. She looked at him and asked, "How do you do it?"

"How do I do what?"

"Escape the guilt."

"Ah. Well, to be honest, I haven't quite figured out how to do that. My grandmother told me several years ago that this would happen when I decided to release my heart to love again. She said it would be up to me if I let guilt hold me prisoner, or if I stepped out in faith and took a chance on love again."

"So, you're saying we're in the same position?"

"If you're trying to figure out if taking a chance on me is worth it, then yes."

Claire nodded and then told him, "I don't think that helps much."

Travis smiled, "Let's go find a tree and think about happier things. The rest will work itself out, we just need to be willing to try and let go of the past. The future is bright, I can see it."

* * *

An hour later...

As Travis watched Tyler and Claire interact with one another, he became more sure than ever that Claire was in their lives for a reason. He needed her laughter and smile, and she needed him to give her a reason to smile.

"We found a tree," she told him breathlessly, her cheeks rosy with the cold and her snow hat slightly askew from tussling with his son.

"Good. I was starting to think we came out here for a snowball fight, not to find a Christmas tree," Travis told her with a chuckle. When she picked up a handful of snow and lobbed it at him, he leered at her teasingly and made a production of picking up his own handful. He packed it down, making it into a perfectly shaped ball and then held it up for her to see.

"You wanna play with the big boys?"

Claire eyed the snowball and then leaned down and whispered something to Tyler. His son gave a whoop of delight and charged off around the corner. Claire waited a few second and then smirked at Travis. "Sure. When you find some, send them my way." With that, she picked up a quick handful of snow and tossed it at him, then bolted after his son.

Travis chuckled and lobbed the snowball after her, but it fell at her feet. He picked up more snow and trailed after her, frowning when he rounded the corner of the trees and saw neither Claire nor his son. He took a few more steps into the clearing, and then with a whoop of delight, snowballs rained down upon him.

Tyler's screams of delight were worth every speck of snow that found its way inside Travis's collars. He returned the favor,

170

hastily forming snowballs and tossing them in the general direction from whence he was being attacked. He thought he was getting the upper hand when the barrage of snow stopped, so he slowly edged his way forward.

Tyler's giggle gave his son away. Travis whirled around just as Tyler launched himself at his father's legs. Travis caught him in his arms and swung him up into the air, the snowballs in his son's hands falling down in his face, as he sputtered and tried not to drop the little boy.

"Whoa," Travis exclaimed, bringing Tyler down to his side and holding him like a sack of potatoes. "Did you put him up to that?"

Claire was laughing and nodding. "Your expression when that snow fell in your face…"

Travis narrowed his eyes at her and then set Tyler down and whispered in his ear. Tyler eagerly nodded and then took off running for Claire. She caught him when he hugged her knees. She tousled his hair, praising him for being so stealthy.

Travis took advantage of her distraction and slipped around the trees to make his way up behind her. When she looked up and saw he was missing, she asked, "Tyler, where did your daddy go?"

"I'm right here," he whispered from directly behind her. He lifted a hand filled with snow in front of her face. She shrieked and tried to back away, only he was right there. A solid wall of flesh barred her escape. "No so fast. I think you should apologize for teaching my son to throw snow at his father."

Claire laughed and shook her head. "I'm not sorry."

Travis laughed with her and then nodded at Tyler who released her legs and backed up, clapping his hands when Travis picked Claire up and headed for a nearby snowbank. "I bet I can change your mind."

She stopped laughing as they neared the pile of snow. Clinging to his shoulders, she asked, "You wouldn't really toss me in the snow, right?"

Travis wiggled his eyebrows at her and then bent down and kissed her on the nose. "Are you ready to apologize yet?"

Claire nodded. "Yes. I'm deeply sorry for teaching your son how to best his father at snowball fighting. I'd be happy to give you a few pointers, so you'll do better next time."

Travis laughed, a deep belly laugh as she twisted, sending them both down into the snowbank. She shrieked as the snow found its way against her skin. He rolled so that she was lying on top of him and not the icy snow. "Sorry about that. I really didn't intend for us both to end up in the snow."

Claire smiled down at him and then her expression froze, as did his own. The air around them seemed to settle. It was as if they were the only two people on earth. She looked into his eyes, and he brushed hair off her cheek. Her snow hat had come off at some point.

"What are we doing here?" she whispered.

"Getting to know one another," Travis whispered back. "You okay?"

"I think so. It's been so long since…"

"For me, too. We can take this as slow as we need to, but I want you to know that I'm falling for you."

"How can you know that? You've only known me a few days."

"Call it intuition, but I can feel it." Travis placed his hand on his heart. "Here."

"Daddy! Claire! I wanna play, too." Tyler climbed on top of Claire, and the moment was lost. Travis extricated himself and his son from Claire and then pulled her to her feet.

"Let's get that tree cut down and take it home. We'll have to decorate it tomorrow, but since we have the next four days off, we should have plenty of time."

"Can Claire come?" Tyler asked.

"Claire is going to come and sleep over at our house for a few days. What do you think about that, Tyler?"

"Yay!"

Travis shared a smile with his son and then nudged Claire. "That gets a Yay from me, too." He rubbed his hands together and then signaled for the tree lot man to bring the ATV and the saw. "Let's get this done and go get some hot chocolate."

He watched Claire pull Tyler a safe distance away while the tree was cut down and lifted onto the trailer. She was so good with his son; he could easily imagine what kind of mother she'd been before the tragedy. She was an amazing woman. She wasn't Emily, but no one would ever compare to her. Emily had been his first love, but he was starting to believe that she wasn't meant to be his only love.

He could easily see himself building a future with Claire. True, he didn't know her all that well, but what he did know about her assured him that she was a woman he wanted to spend the next fifty years unraveling. If anyone had told him he could begin to fall in love in such a short period of time, Travis would have laughed at them.

With Emily, falling in love had been a slow and gradual

process. They'd been young and friends long before they'd decided to let romance enter their relationship. Travis had thought that was how love developed. Meeting Claire had him rethinking everything he'd thought he knew about relationships.

Claire stirred his soul, brought out his protective instincts, and he found himself looking for ways to make her smile. When she did, it was if the sun became electrified. She brought light into his life. It complimented the light that came from Tyler and others in his life. She filled the empty space in his soul that had been left when he put his late wife in the ground.

Now, if he could just not scare her off by coming across too serious too quickly. Claire had been running from her past for a long time and needed space; an opportunity to heal. He'd stay by her side, being supportive and slowly wooing her into a relationship. When the time was right, he'd make sure she knew exactly how he felt.

Claire was his Christmas miracle. She'd made him believe in the possibility of love after tragic loss. She'd shown him that his heart had healed, and she inspired him to live for the here and now as well as the future. Travis was done being tied down to memories of the past.

***

Hope was so happy, she flew up into the clouds and did somersaults, as she rejoiced in Travis's newfound attitude. Her mission had been to help him open his heart up to love again. He'd just done that, mostly on his own.

The power of the human heart to heal itself and the capacity of it to love was a miracle in itself. Hope was thrilled to bear witness to the miracle of love and couldn't wait to share the news of her success with her friends and Matthias.

She headed toward the heavenly realm. Choir practice was about to start, and she'd never felt more like rejoicing than now. Hopefully, she'd be celebrating Claire's renewed lease on life in the next day or two as well.

She entered the choir room and immediately joined in the final chorus of *Joy to the World*. She looked for both Charity and Joy, but neither of them had shown up for practice. Hope spent a few minutes with the other angels, then she headed back down to Earth. Hopefully, her friends were having just as much success as she was at the moment.

Chapter 21

Later that evening…

Claire walked around the department store's second floor, nodding to employees she knew and keeping an eye out for Alex. She and Travis had arrived with Tyler in tow. Travis had made sure he kept her by his side while introducing her to his parents, his grandmother, and the board of directors and their wives. Claire's nerves had been strung tight, but as the evening progressed, she'd started to relax. Until she'd spied Alex across the way and realized he'd been observing her.

She'd turned him down for the Christmas party several times and, by the look on his face, he wasn't happy about being thrown over for the boss. Claire thought about trying to explain things to him, but knowing Alex, that would only add fuel to the fire. She had a sneaky suspicion that some of the rumors mulling around the water dispensers came directly from his lips. Alex was someone she most definitely didn't want to cross swords with. Not right now.

She moved about, stopping to chat with Becky and then again with Amy. Tyler was keeping her little girls' company in the elves' workshop. Claire had to give high marks to whomever had planned this year's event. They had done a magnificent job of including activities that were age appropriate for everyone.

"Having a good time?" Alex's voice came from behind her.

Claire mentally sighed and then pasted on a smile and turned around. "I don't normally attend these things, but so far, it appears to be going well."

"I saw you come in with Mr. Hammerstein. I didn't realize you'd decided to skip the middlemen and go straight to the top,"

Alex told her with a slight sneer in his voice.

"Excuse me?" Claire replied.

"You heard me. I guess my pay grade wasn't quite high enough."

"Alex, your status with the company had nothing to do with why I didn't want to go out with you," Claire tried to explain.

"Really? From where I'm standing that's exactly what it looks like."

Claire shook her head at him sadly. "Think what you want. I need to go find Travis. We have a childcare center to reveal."

"So, the rumors are true. You and the boss are an item?"

Claire eyed him and shook her head. "I shouldn't even bother responding to that remark, but I will anyway. You've known me long enough to know that I don't indulge in the rumor mill. I don't listen to it, and I certainly won't be responsible for contributing to it." She turned on her heel and walked away, hurrying toward the customer service desk and hoping she could find a few minutes of solitude before she had to deal with anyone again. Alex was like a bad penny—he just wouldn't go away.

She pushed open the door, swiped her card key through the lock, and then headed down the stairs to her darkened office. She sank down in one of the large overstuffed chairs, not even bothering to turn the lights on. She sat there for the longest time, listening to the muted sounds of the party going on. She closed her eyes for a minute, blinking them rapidly when a soft male voice called her name.

"Claire, it's time to wake up. We have people wanting to see the center."

She blinked up into the eyes of Travis and frowned. "I was

having a really good dream."

"Oh yeah?"

"I was on a beach, sleeping beneath the sun, and no one was rude enough to wake me up."

"I wasn't being rude. I was just doing what was required. I didn't think you wanted me to parade the employees past your office while you were napping in it."

"No. No, that wouldn't be appropriate. What time is it?"

"Nearly eight o'clock," Travis confirmed.

"Okay, I'm awake. Let's go turn on the lights and bring some employees through. I had Linda, one of the new girls hired to man the reception desk, print up some extra forms so that parents can register their kids tonight if they so choose."

"Wonderful idea. That will help us with knowing how many people we need to adequately staff the center."

"That was my thought as well." Claire stood up, smoothed a hand down the gold dress and then stretched her arms above her head briefly. "Let's go do this."

When she looked at Travis, he was staring at her with a peculiar look on his face. She had to ask, "Is everything alright?"

"Do you have any idea how beautiful you are?" he asked reverently.

Claire blushed and shook her head. "We should probably head upstairs."

Travis shook his head and approached her. "Not before I do this," he tipped her chin up and lowered his lips to hers. He kissed her with passion and a hint of possession, and Claire soaked up his attentions. Each time they kissed, she reacted more strongly to his presence. It was thrilling and amazing, but also confusing. Yet, she wouldn't trade kissing Travis for anything in the world.

Travis broke the kiss and then pulled her by the hand to the upstairs doors. They greeted everyone, then proceeded to escort them in groups of twenty people through the facility. This continued for more than two hours before they finally had a small break.

The only blemish upon the evening came when Alex showed up for a tour and insisted on Claire being the leader of his group. She smiled and agreed to do so, but the entire time they were walking through the facility, Alex kept standing too close and attempting to separate her from the others. When they reached the large playground area, she invited everyone to take a few minutes and wander around before meeting her back at the entrance when they were ready to head back.

Alex refused to check out the playground. Instead, he remained by her side, continuing his dialogue from before.

"I wish you would have at least given me a shot. Or had the courtesy to be honest with me and just tell me I wasn't good enough for you," he whined.

Claire had reached her tolerance limit. She turned to face him with her hands on her hips. "Alex, you have no one but yourself to blame for what I'm about to say. I have tried to be congenial and nice to you, but you just don't seem to be taking a hint. So, let me be very clear here. I never agreed to date you. I have no intention of ever dating you. Ever.

"There is no connection, or whatever it is you've convinced yourself, between us. We happen to work for the same company, and from here on out, if you don't keep your distance, I will have no other choice but to file a complaint with human resources over your harassment."

She could tell by his expression that she'd just made an enemy, but Claire was tired of being quiet and just letting life go on around her. Travis had awakened her to the fact that she was young and still had a lot of life in her. She was going to do it on her terms. Alex and any others who would come after him simply needed to listen.

"You can be a real b—"

"I wouldn't finish that word if I were you," Travis told him in a low, angry voice from just behind her shoulder.

She turned her head and was slightly taken aback by the look on Travis's face. He was furious and making no attempt to hide that fact. "Travis…"

He shook his head and then moved her to the side, stepping in front of her and blocking her from Alex's view. "I will personally escort you out of the building if you even think of harassing Claire again. Do I make myself clear?"

She heard Alex murmur his agreement before he hurried out of the space. When Travis turned back to her, she said, "Thank you for that."

"No problem. You were doing a fine job on your own, but no employee is going to talk in a derogatory manner to another employee. Not on the premises. Not and keep their job."

"Alex is nothing more than a nuisance. He's been asking me out for months, and I always turn him down. He felt as if you beat him to the chase, and I chose you over him."

"You did, didn't you?" Travis asked with a smirk.

Claire rolled her eyes and nodded. "I guess so." She raised her voice and announced that the tour was returning to the front desk in two minutes.

"You do that well," Travis complimented her.

"It takes practice, but sometimes the best way to calm a crowd is to give them a specific task with a timeline for them to finish. Even adults thrive in structure."

"There's the preschool teacher talking."

Claire smiled and then answered a few questions for those who were gathering to be escorted back. "Is this the last group?"

"You know it. Douglas already took Tyler home. He was falling asleep while talking to Santa."

"Ooh, that can't be good. We'll have to make sure he gets another visit so that doesn't happen."

"My thoughts exactly, but I'm thinking one of the smaller shopping centers closer to home. Let's get these people out of here. I'll go make my 'thank you for coming' speech and tell them how to pick up their Christmas bonuses. Then, we are free to leave. My parents and grandmother will hold down the fort while we slip away."

"That sounds like a really sound plan. My feet are killing me," she complained softly, as they began to lead the group back to the front of the center.

Claire made small talk while Travis went to the center of the store and climbed up on the platform that had been erected just for this event. The store had closed early and then a team of hired workers had come in and transformed it into an elegant party, complete with a buffet and plenty of seating.

A similar crew had been hired to come in after midnight and make sure everything was cleaned up and returned to its normal position before the store opened in the morning. Travis had insisted that the company party was intended to be enjoyed by all and, if some of their workers were responsible for set-up or teardown, they wouldn't enjoy attending nearly as much. Claire and Amy had both agreed.

Claire listened as Travis greeted everyone and then talked about the decision that had been made to put more bonus money into the employees' pockets this year. In previous years, the grand ballroom at the Four Seasons Hotel had been rented out—at a hefty price tag—to host the Hammerstein company Christmas party. Travis believed the employees would rather have more cash in their bonuses than a fancy place for a party. He was right.

"I'm happy to report that, by hosting our own Christmas party, every employee will be receiving an additional bonus this year."

Cheers and claps accompanied his announcement and, after thanking the board of directors and his family, Travis wished everyone a Merry Christmas and promised to see them all December 26th. He invited them all to enjoy the live music that had been brought in for the evening and to make sure they stopped by and talked to Santa before heading home for the evening. Santa, it seemed, had been talked into holding everyone's bonus checks. Anyone who didn't pick it up in person this evening would be receiving it electronically in the morning.

Claire smiled at people, as Travis led her toward the elevator half-an-hour later. She'd enjoyed meeting his family, especially his grandmother, and wasn't surprised when she all but demanded Claire's presence at Christmas dinner. Claire had promised to be there and had earned a speculative look from the older woman when Travis had slipped an arm around her waist shortly thereafter.

"Are you glad you came now?" Travis inquired, as he led her to the shiny sports car parked beneath the store.

"I have to admit it was more fun than I'd thought it would be."

"Good. The employees seemed happy with my decision."

"Everyone can use additional money this time of year. I don't think anyone minded not having the party at a fancy hotel. This was a little more laidback and they were able to bring their children. You made a good decision."

"Thank you for that vote of confidence. Now, was there anything else you needed to grab from your apartment before we head out. I'm hoping I don't have to drive back into the city for the next four days."

"I think I'm fine. I packed several changes of clothes, my laptop, and some other things I might need."

"Home it is, then."

Chapter 22

Travis exited the parking garage, his space protected by a separate automatic door so that he never had to worry about someone besides himself parking there. He headed down Michigan Avenue and eventually they made their way out to the highway, heading away from the lights of the city and to the place Claire was going to call home for the next few days.

Just thinking about that brought butterflies to life in her stomach. She clenched her hands together in her lap and gave herself a stern talking to.

I'm doing this because I like Travis and want to find out if there's anything between the two of us, just like he wants to. This is a good thing, and I won't be alone at Christmas.

"Why don't you find something on the radio for us to listen to? With the snow starting to come down, we have at least a forty-five-minute drive ahead of us."

Claire nodded and then turned on the radio, slowly moving through the channels until she came to a soft rock station that was playing non-stop Christmas carols, many of which were only the instrumental versions. Her favorite kind.

"Christmas music?" Travis asked in shock.

Claire shrugged. "I can change it…"

"No. No, I just thought you didn't like it."

"You know why I felt that way, but for some reason, it kind of brings me comfort. Reminds me of all the years before the tragic one. They were good. It's strange how one bad event can wipe away multiple years of good ones."

"Only for a short time and only for as long as it's allowed to have that power. I'm glad you're remembering the good times. Want to tell me some of them?"

Claire nodded and shared stories from her childhood and the early years of her marriage. It felt good to think about those times, and even when she remembered the one that had changed her life so dramatically, it was with a sadness she could handle instead of the soul-wrenching grief from before. She was letting go.

They reached Travis's house and were greeted by Douglas and the news that Tyler had finally told Santa what he wanted for Christmas. A puppy.

"Great," Travis groaned in response.

"And on that note, have a good night. Claire." Douglas gave Travis a mock salute and headed off to his own quarters on the other side of the house.

"A puppy?" Claire whispered, as they headed for the family room at the back of the house, far away from Tyler's bedroom.

"He's been wanting one for a while now, and I keep putting him off. Guess my time's run out."

Claire nodded and then asked the million-dollar question. "Where are you going to find a puppy this close to Christmas?"

Travis smiled at her as they settled on the couches, and he picked up the television controller. "That's where you're going to be amazed at my forethought. I've been speaking to a breeder for the last few months. She has a litter of Golden Retriever pups ready to go. She's holding one of them for me, I just have to let her know by the twenty-third if it's going to happen."

"Guess you'd better contact her first thing in the morning, huh?" Claire asked with a twinkle in her eye. She toed off her heels

185

and then groaned as her feet sunk into the plush carpet. "I hate wearing heels, just for the record."

Travis was watching her and then he glanced up at the clock over the mantle. "How about I go rustle us up some snacks and you can change out of that dress. It's gorgeous on you but doesn't really look all that comfortable."

"About as comfortable right now as the shoes." Claire stood up, picked up her shoes and then wandered back down the hallway. She'd unpacked her belongings early this afternoon before getting ready for the party. She changed into a pair of soft sweatpants and a t-shirt, then pulled on a soft cardigan over it. She wandered back toward the kitchen twenty minutes later, feeling much more relaxed.

Travis had changed as well and was wearing a pair of fleece pajama pants and a long-sleeved Henley. "Have a seat. I made us some popcorn and raided the candy jar."

"Popcorn and candy. Sounds like you read my mind," Claire told him.

Travis picked up the remote and then asked, "Christmas movie or something else?"

"What's playing?"

Travis scrolled through the channels and then smiled, "*White Christmas*. Feel like a little Bing Crosby and Rosemary Clooney?"

"That's one of my all-time favorites. That and *It's A Wonderful Life*. Some of the newer movies are good as well, but I kind of like the old classics."

"I agree." Travis started the movie, and Claire settled back to watch. The storyline was one she knew by heart, but it was the choreography, singing and dancing that always drew her in. "The people who made these movies were very talented."

Two hours later, the movie ended, and Claire could feel her eyelids starting to droop. "I should head to bed while I still can."

"It's been a long couple of days. We don't have much to do tomorrow besides decorate the tree and relax. You can sleep in as long as you like."

"I will definitely take you up on that offer. Most mornings, I'm up before five so that I can get a little housework done before I leave to catch the train into the city."

"Sleep as late as you like. I'll do my best to keep Tyler from disturbing you."

Claire nodded and headed for the hallway, only to find Travis had beat her to it as she said goodnight.

Travis smiled down at her and then turned her so that she was facing him. He slowly wrapped his arms around her waist, giving her plenty of time to pull away if she wanted to, but she was exactly where she wanted to be.

"Let's try that again," he whispered as he trailed his lips over her forehead and down her cheek. They ended on her lips. She kissed him back, her body moving even closer to absorb his warmth.

"That's how to say goodnight," he whispered, as he trailed his lips down her neck and to the curve where it met her shoulder.

"I like your way better than mine," she whispered, going up on her tiptoes and turning his head back so that their lips met again. She kissed him this time, memorizing the feel of his lips beneath her own and the way they seemed to fit together like a custom-made puzzle.

When she broke away from him, she was out of breath, but he was in no better shape and that made her smile.

"Goodnight," she whispered and then ducked around him

and headed for her borrowed bedroom. She didn't trust herself if she stayed there any longer. She was just beginning to process the fact that her heart was still alive, and she needed to take things slowly.

She had a hard time going to sleep, and when her dreams arrived, she woke disappointed because Scott hadn't been in them. She so badly wished she could talk to him, even if just through his headstone. She needed to tell him what she was feeling and somehow, feel like he was okay with her moving on. The voice in her head had told her it was, but it wasn't enough.

Sleep finally claimed her and she woke in the morning, slightly depressed, but also looking forward to spending the day with Travis and Tyler. She was going to make this a good Christmas, even if she had to force herself to smile. Maybe if she faked it long enough, she'd eventually believe that things were going to get better.

Chapter 23

Christmas Eve…

Travis watched as Claire helped Tyler roll out the gingerbread dough. The house was decorated for the holidays and now they were making gingerbread cookies. Claire had confessed that, while she loved gingerbread, a house made out of the delectable treat was more than she was capable of pulling off. With the help of a cookie cutter, she could just manage gingerbread men.

Tyler had been ecstatic with the idea of decorating the cookies and Travis smiled as he realized his son was wearing as much frosting as the cookies were. "Tyler, buddy, the frosting goes on the cookies, not you."

"He'll clean up," Claire interjected.

"I know." Travis watched her pipe frosting around the edge of the cookie and then begin filling it in. "You're pretty good at that."

"Thanks. Decorating cookies is like a needed skill when you work with preschoolers. They love to decorate cookies for every season and every holiday. Sugar cookie dough is cheap to make and a fun treat for the kids to take home."

"You've missed doing this," Travis surmised.

"Yeah. I have. I was just fooling myself that I could lock this part of me away forever. I have you to thank for bringing me back out into the light."

"You are very welcome. So, I spoke to the breeder a few minutes ago and they will have a special package for us to pick up on our way home from Christmas dinner."

189

Claire grinned at him. "He's going to be super excited."

"Yeah, which is why we'll pick the critter up on the way home. I don't want to be responsible for ruining my grandmother's Persian rugs."

"I think that's a very wise idea. These last few days have been wonderful. Thank you for inviting me to spend this time with you and your son."

"I was just thinking the same thing. After Tyler goes to bed tonight, I was hoping maybe you could help me finish wrapping presents? Before we go to midnight mass?"

"I'd love to." Travis had told her about the midnight mass held on Christmas Eve at a local church he'd been attending and had asked her if she wanted to go. God had been another thing Claire had tried to forget the last four years, and since returning from Winchester, she'd found herself talking to him more than once a day. It seemed like she'd walked away from everyone and everything that could have helped her heal so much sooner. She pushed those thoughts aside. There was no way to undo the past and she was determined to make the future better.

"Tyler doesn't go to mass with you?"

"Not just yet. It's kind of late for him, and I don't want a cranky kid tomorrow."

"Now, that I can agree with. I'd love to help you wrap things."

Claire had a few things to wrap of her own. While Travis and Tyler had been out shoveling snow the day before, Douglas had driven Claire into the closest suburb, complete with plenty of shopping choices. She'd selected gifts for all three men and picked up a nice housewarming present for his grandmother. She hoped everyone liked what she'd picked out for them, but then reminded

190

herself it was the thought that counted, not the gift itself.

For Douglas, she'd gotten the latest video game. She'd been surprised to find out that he was an avid gamer. She'd taken time finding out what kind of games he liked. For Tyler, she'd gotten some learning toys that she'd known he didn't have. He was a bright little boy and his mind needed to be kept active. She got him a couple of wooden puzzles and some paper and crayons.

She'd struggled with what to get Travis. He was the man who had everything, and she struggled to find something she could give him that he wouldn't already have three of or never use. She'd wandered into a lovely knitting shop on her venture and had known right away what his gift would be.

She'd picked out yarn, needles, and a few other items she needed and then hidden it until she'd gotten into her borrowed room at the house. For the last two nights, and for a short time each morning, she'd been working on her gift for him. She'd finished it a little earlier that afternoon while Tyler was taking a short nap and Travis was dealing with some business matters. He'd thought she was in her room resting, but she'd been putting the final touches on the scarf and hat she was making him.

"I have a few things to wrap as well. Maybe I'll do those in my bedroom and then come out and join you?" she suggested.

"You could go wrap them now, if you like, and I'll keep Tyler occupied."

Claire nodded and then grabbed some wrapping paper, the scissors, and a roll of tape and carried them to her room. She wrapped everything up and then left it lying on her bed. She took a moment before leaving her bedroom to offer up a silent prayer to the heavens.

She'd been happy these last few days. She'd brought along a

box full of Scott's papers to go through in her free time. Last night, she'd found a letter he'd written to her almost a year before his death. He'd been flying to a conference and had been worried about something happening to him. He'd written her his final goodbye letter, and as she'd read it, she'd realized it could have been written the day he died. It probably would have read the exact same.

Scott had been a very consistent man and his feelings were never in question. After reading his letter, she'd known that he'd wanted her to move on with her life and find someone else to love and share this journey with. Not because he didn't love her, but because he did and only wanted the best for her. She knew, after reading his words, that he would be more than okay with her having feelings for Travis and seeing if they had a future together.

Father God, I know I probably don't even deserve to have you listen to me, but I could use a little help down here. I like Travis, but I'm not even over losing Scott and my children. How can I possibly be thinking about having a relationship with another man and his son? It feels disloyal, but only when I'm alone with too much time to think.

Maybe you could give me a sign or something? Thank you for the dream. I know I probably should have thanked you before now, but better late than never, right? Anyway, thank you. I needed to know that they were okay, and that Scott knew about Rachel.

She read the letter one more time while Tyler was being put down to bed. When she joined Travis in the family room an hour later, she was filled with confidence and something to prove. To herself and to him. She was developing feelings for Travis, and she wasn't willing to wait and see if they were real. She wanted to know now.

They were both aware of just how short life could be. Claire wanted to take it by the horns and conquer this niggling of fear that she felt every time she thought about having a future with Travis. It was silly, and Claire wasn't going to be controlled by it any longer.

***

Christmas Eve in Heaven

"*Hallelujah! Let Heaven and Earth Rejoice! Christ the newborn King is born in Bethlehem! Glory in the Highest! Peace on the Earth!*"

The angel choir finished the song with their wings and arms uplifted, their voices raised as they proclaimed the arrival of Christmas. A glow from the palace in the center of Heaven had them all beaming at a job well done as God and His Son showed their approval.

"Hope smiled and then headed out of the arena with Joy and Charity by her side.

"I've got to get back," Joy told them.

"What's the hurry? It's Christmas Eve."

"I want to watch and see how everything turns out," she replied.

"Me too," Charity nodded. She'd been the most secretive of the three, and Claire couldn't wait to find out what kind of stress her friend had been through.

"Guess I'll see you both later."

She took a moment to speak with the choir director before she headed back down to Earth. It was almost midnight and Claire and Travis had just arrived at the local chapel. The midnight mass was getting ready to start. Hope took up a position in the balcony, ready to enjoy the service.

Chapter 24

Claire sat next to Travis on the pew, her eyes taking in the beautiful pipe organ that occupied the entire front wall. The organist looked so tiny against all of the pipes, and the sounds she was creating were what she imagined Heaven sounded like.

"How long have you been coming here?" Claire asked him quietly.

"Off and on since I was a little boy. My parents lived outside of Chicago until I was seven, and then we started moving around a lot. I usually spent a few months each year here during the summer, and my grandparents always brought me here on Sundays."

"It's lovely. The architecture. The organ. The children's choir. Their voices are magical."

"I agree."

Travis reached for her hand. She let him have it, relaxing and just enjoying the sounds of the holiday season. A beautiful nativity scene was erected in the front of the church. It seemed everyone was full of the spirit of the season this night. She'd had more people wish her a Merry Christmas than ever before.

"I like it here," Claire told him, as the service wound to an end.

"I'm glad. You're welcome to come with Tyler and I any Sunday you like, or every Sunday would be my preference."

Claire was quiet until they reached the car and then she told him, "I didn't realize how much I missed church until tonight. Thank you for taking me."

"Thank you for going with me. My grandmother will probably give us both the third- degree tomorrow."

"She was there?" Claire asked in surprise.

"She never misses a midnight mass. She was seated down in the third row with my parents. She claims that is her pew and no one besides God himself would dare sit there."

"Is it really her pew?" Claire asked, knowing a few people from Winchester who acted like they had their own private pews, so no one else was allowed to sit there.

"Actually, I believed they did put a Hammerstein name plate on the pew after my grandfather died."

"Ah. Well, then she's justified. Will she be put out that you didn't go up and say hello?"

"Not at all."

Claire was surprised to find they were pulling into the garage at his house. She hid a yawn behind her hand. "I didn't realize I was so tired. What time is it?"

"Almost one o'clock in the morning. Tyler will be up by six, unless we're unlucky and then he might be up by five."

"Great," Claire said, frowning. "I remember those days and closing bedroom doors, turning off alarms and such, just trying to get Daniel to sleep in on Christmas morning until a respectable time. Seven. Eight. Nine would have been my preference, but I was never that lucky."

"Me neither. Even when Tyler was a baby, he rarely slept more than three hours at a time. What about Daniel? Was he a sleeper, or an eater?"

"An eater? Every two or three hours around the clock. I finally gave in the third day home from the hospital and took him into bed with me." She pulled a face, before adding, "He was still wanting to sleep in our bed when he turned two. We finally had to just weather a few nights of tears and tantrums before he

195

experienced the joys of having his own bed. That first night where I got to sleep all night without having little elbows and knees hitting me all night was a taste of heaven on earth."

Travis chuckled and then turned off the car and shut the garage door. "Come on, you look like you're about ready to drop."

"Almost." Claire entered the house before him and headed for her room. She turned to call back a goodnight and…

"Oomph!" She bumped her nose into his chest. He'd been following closely behind her.

"Steady there," Travis whispered. He smoothed her hair back and then searched her eyes. "I really enjoyed today. I know I should probably wait to say this, but I've learned that life moves fast and sometimes you don't get a second chance to say things. Best to get them out right away."

Claire felt her heart clench at the look in his eyes. She opened her mouth to say something, but he stopped her with a finger on her lips.

"Let me say this, please?"

Claire nodded, and he smiled softly at her. His thumb was brushing a path back and forth on her cheek. She leaned into his touch before she could even think about the wisdom of doing such.

"Claire, I said this once before, but there is something about you that calls to me. After Emily died, I was sure I would never want another relationship. It just hurt too badly to lose her, and I never wanted to go through that again. I probably would have hidden away like you did if I hadn't had Tyler and a family that nagged me on a consistent basis until I started living again.

"Anyway, I took this job because I've learned that, if I keep busy, I'm not so lonely. Every time I saw an attractive woman and even thought about asking her out, I would be bombarded by this guilt that I was being unfaithful to Emily.

"You told me you were feeling the same way. I think it's just something that happens when you lose a spouse. It doesn't mean that being attracted to someone else, or even falling in love with them, is wrong; it's just another part of the letting-go process."

Travis paused and then smiled at her, "Claire St. Peters, you've brought my heart back to life these last few days. I don't want this to end after tomorrow. I want you to stay close so that we can continue to learn about one another and see where this leads. Tell me you feel at least a small fraction of that?"

Claire nodded. "I do feel the chemistry, and yesterday I was afraid of it. I felt like I was being unfaithful to Scott's memory, but then I found a letter he wrote me a year before he died. He was travelling for work and, for some reason, he was nervous about something happening to him and leaving Daniel and I all alone. In his letter, he told me he didn't want me to spend my life all alone while mourning him. He wanted me to let love find me again and give the next man in my life just as much of my heart as I'd given him."

Travis shook his head, "Scott sounds like an amazing man. Emily didn't write me a note, but she made me promise on her deathbed that I wouldn't stay single. I guess I haven't done such a good job of keeping that promise."

"You told me that everyone grieves in their own way, and there is no right or wrong; there just is."

"I did say that, didn't I? Guess I should start listening to my own counsel."

Claire smile at him. "I think we've both had love. We know what it feels like and that it takes work. We're realists because we know that it doesn't always last."

"But does that mean we hide our heads in the sand and stay

single for the rest of our lives? I can't do that. I don't think you want to do that, either. We're good together, Claire. The last few days have proven that. I know it's too soon to ask you for a commitment, but I firmly believe that commitment is in our future. Right now, I'm just asking you to consider extending our time together, so that we can truly get to know one another."

"So, what are you asking me? To date you? Have lunch with you in the employee lounge?"

"I'm asking you to date me. Have dinner with me. Go out with me and to Tyler's school functions. Be a part of my life and let me be part of yours. I know just enough about you to know I want to learn everything there is." Travis paused and shook his head, "I wondered if it was too soon to say these things."

"I don't think it is," Claire told him. She reached up and cupped his cheek, searching his eyes before rising up on her tiptoes and kissing him softly on the lips. "I feel the same way, and I learned the hard way that there is no promise of tomorrow. There's today and, if you don't make every moment count, you could get left behind."

"What are you saying?" Travis asked.

"I'm saying that I want the same thing you do, but I don't want to waste a lot of time trying to figure out if it's perfect. Relationships take work, and I feel like we've already shared so much. We know each other better than some couples who have been married for twenty years."

Travis nodded and then kissed her. "I think I get where you're headed with this, and I agree. Spend the rest of the year here with Tyler and I and, if we still feel this way on New Year's Eve, I say we get married and move on with the rest of our lives."

"That's faster than I might have had in mind, but…yes. I'll stay in your guest bedroom until New Year's Eve, then we can reevaluate where this is headed."

"Be warned," Travis told her. "If we decide to get married, we'll be getting on the company jet and heading straight for Las Vegas before morning is over."

"That works for me. I had a big wedding once; I don't need another."

They stared at one another, and she whispered, "Did we really just have a conversation about our wedding?"

"We did. I think we should probably call it a night, don't you?"

Claire nodded, "Most definitely."

Travis kissed her once more before stepping back to open up the bedroom door for her. "Goodnight, Claire. Sweet dreams for the few hours you have left."

"You as well."

Claire slipped into the bedroom and got ready for bed, her mind spinning with the discussion she'd just had. They'd basically just agreed to get married if they still liked one another come New Year's Eve.

Talk about jumping the gun.

As Claire drifted off to sleep, she couldn't stop thinking about Travis and a speedy wedding. She'd been to Las Vegas once, so she had no trouble envisioning the bright lights and garish displays. She chuckled as she made a promise to herself.

"If I end up getting married again in Las Vegas, none other than Elvis himself is going to do the honors."

Chapter 25

Christmas Day...

"Claire, I hope you won't be a stranger," Greta Hammerstein told her, as she and Travis prepared to leave later in the afternoon. Douglas had taken Tyler with him, giving Travis and Claire time to go pick up the puppy that was being held for them.

"I'll bring her with me again, I promise," Travis hugged his grandmother. "Merry Christmas."

"Merry Christmas to you as well. Bring Tyler by next week so that he can show me his new puppy."

"Are you sure? Puppies can make some pretty big messes."

"I'm sure. I'll see you then."

Travis and Claire were laughing, as they pulled away from the Hammerstein Estate. "I can't believe my grandmother wants a new puppy running around her house."

"Your grandmother is wonderful."

"Did you ever meet your grandparents?"

"Sadly, no. But I enjoyed meeting her and your parents."

"They enjoyed meeting you again as well. Now, we're looking for..."

"That little house right there with the puppies for sale sign?"

"That would be it."

Thirty minutes later they were driving home, a golden bundle of fur curled up in Claire's lap. "Tyler is going to be so excited."

"Yeah. I'm thinking no one is going to get any sleep tonight."

"They might surprise you. They've both had big days."

Travis drove them to the house and then came around and took the puppy from Claire's arms. "I'm going to take him into the family room. Can you find Tyler and bring him in there?"

"Sure thing."

Minutes later, Claire and Tyler entered the family room. Travis had placed the puppy inside a closed basket and had tied a large red bow on the handle.

"Tyler, are you ready for the next part of your present?"

"More presents?" Tyler asked, clapping his hands and running to stand in front of his father. "I like Christmas."

"I'm sure you do," Travis told him in a quiet voice meant for Claire's ears. He set the basket down and then invited Tyler to open it carefully.

"A puppy!" Tyler's scream awakened the puppy and, after cowering in the corner of the basket for a moment, the puppy decided Tyler looked like a good playmate. He started yipping and trying to climb out of the basket.

Travis lifted him out and then sat back and watched Tyler and the puppy get acquainted. Claire joined him on the couch a few moments later, having taken some video on her phone to commemorate the moment. Travis lifted his arm and placed it around her shoulders and, when she relaxed against his side, it felt like home. She felt so right sitting next to him, and Travis felt more blessed than ever.

"Today has been another amazing day," he murmured in her ear.

"Thank you," Claire told him. "Are you ready for tomorrow?"

"As ready as I'll ever be. How many children do you think will show up?"

"There will be eighty employees tomorrow and most of them have at least one child."

"That could mean a lot of traffic. How many kids can we legally have in the center?"

"It depends on their ages. The younger they are, the smaller the student to teacher ratio becomes. I should have already done this, but there were so many other things needing done first. I'll post a list at the check-in desk and in each classroom so that everyone knows how many children can be in each room and how many teachers are needed for the number of children."

"I think we'll have lots of bugs to work out over the next few days."

"I agree."

By this time, both Tyler and the puppy had grown tired and were lying on the floor with the boy's arms curled around the body of the dog. The puppy was so trusting.

"They're going to be best friends," Travis whispered. "I'm not psychic, but I can see into my son's future, and this dog is going to be his constant companion."

"I think that's awesome. Scott was allergic to dogs, so we couldn't have any. I always had dogs growing up."

"I did as well. Sadly, my German Shepherd passed away while I was finishing up college."

"I'm sorry. I know what that's like."

"Well, I didn't mean to turn this conversation sideways. Did you enjoy today? And you're free to tell me if they made you feel uncomfortable."

"Your family was very nice and welcoming."

Travis laughed softly. "I'll pass along the compliment."

They lapsed into a friendly silence, as they watched the boy and his new dog. There was no noise, just the ticking of the clock on top of the mantle. The only lights were those from the Christmas tree. A sense of rightness and peace settled over them all, and it was the perfect ending to a perfect Christmas. As perfect of a Christmas as Claire could remember having experienced.

"You're a wonderful father," she murmured to Travis.

"What brought that on?" he queried.

Claire shrugged. "I don't know. I was sitting here thinking about how the Christmases I've experienced measure up to this one. I couldn't come up with one that made me feel like I feel right now. Peace."

"Isn't that one of the gifts the angels brought to the Earth with their announcement?"

"I don't know. I think so."

"Well," Travis stretched his arms and then once again dropped one of them over her shoulders. "I personally like to think that we have angels looking out for us."

Claire yawned and realized she was completely exhausted. "I'm ready for bed."

"I think we could all use an early night. I'll take care of Tyler and put the puppy away in the bathroom for the night."

"Want some help?" Claire asked.

"No. I've got it. Tyler needs a sponge bath before bed tonight. I'll see you in the morning. We'll stop by your apartment after work, and you can grab some fresh clothing."

"I'll be ready. Tomorrow is going to be hectic but hopefully a rewarding day. You should get plenty of rest as well."

"I'm headed there right after depositing him into bed. I'm

going to be hanging out in the childcare center for most of the day. If you need something, I want you to feel free to tell me. I'll either handle it or find someone else who can. I want tomorrow to go as smoothly as possible."

"Me, too. Goodnight." She moved to slid off the couch, but Travis held her in place.

"Is that the best you could do for a goodnight?" he asked teasingly.

Claire blushed and then leaned forward, kissing him softly for a while before pulling back. "Better?"

"Yes, but this is even better." Travis kissed her, deepening the kiss and pouring all of his emotions into the act. Claire could feel his emotions and gave free rein to her own. He broke away long minutes later and whispered, "Merry Christmas."

"Merry Christmas."

Travis released her and she headed for her borrowed bedroom, her heart racing and her skin tingling for long moments after their kiss. She lay in bed, her mind slowly processing the day's events. His family. Their traditions. His kiss. All of it added up to a wonderful holiday that she wouldn't soon forget.

Father God, thank you. I asked for a sign, and maybe I'm reading into things a bit here, but today was so comfortable and easy-going. Despite the chaos of a large dinner and presents being opened. Travis was calm and collected and so patient with his son. Tyler is an adorable little boy and each day I find myself caring more and more for him.

Protect my heart, Lord. If Travis is not the man you have for me to walk through the rest of this life with, please let these feelings for him go away.

Happy Birthday, Jesus. I remember why I loved this holiday so much. Order and symmetry. Merry Christmas.

Chapter 26

New Year's Eve...

Travis watched the woman who had turned his world upside down playing with his son, and the newest member of the family—Tucker. She was so good with both of them, even after spending all day in the childcare center. Today marked the end of the first week since the center opened; it had been a rousing success. They had been almost at capacity each day this week, and Claire had already discussed needing to take childcare needs into consideration when scheduling part-time workers.

Travis had a meeting set up for Claire and the heads of each department on the first Monday of the New Year. He'd watched her this week; she'd smiled more than ever as she got to know the children and watched the center come to life.

"Tyler, time for bed," Travis called out.

"Ah, can't I stay up just a little bit longer?" Tyler whined.

"No. It's a busy day tomorrow, and I want you rested." They were heading to his parents' house as were various other friends and extended family members. Tyler was excited to see his cousins and show them his new puppy. Claire was just glad for a day off. This week at the childcare center had been beyond hectic.

"Come on, squirt," Douglas called from the hallway. "I'll even read you a bedtime story if you like."

Travis kissed his son goodnight and then watched as he hugged Claire and extracted the same from her. "Goodnight, Tyler."

"Night, daddy. Night, Claire."

"Goodnight, Tyler. Sleep tight and don't let the bed bugs bite." She kissed his forehead and off he went, the puppy scrambling to keep up on the slippery tile floors of the hallway.

Travis joined her, scooting close and pulling her against his side. "We're all alone."

"Well, sorta. Tyler could come back down here any moment."

"That's true. Anyway, I thought maybe we could talk about the future."

Claire nodded and then pulled the blanket off the back of the couch and started worrying the fringe. "We work well together."

"Yes, we do. Have you given any thought to what we discussed on Christmas Eve?"

Claire smiled and nodded, "I've given it a great deal of thought. You saved me. I saved you. It seems that we need one another and I, for one, don't want to risk going through this life without you by my side."

"So, are we heading to the airport in the morning instead of New Year's Day brunch?"

"Actually, I have a request. I was in Las Vegas several years before Daniel was born. There was a little white chapel where someone impersonating Elvis performs nightly."

"You are telling me this because why?" Travis asked, but she could tell he was teasing her.

"I have a request. We have to have Elvis perform the ceremony."

"So, we are flying to Las Vegas?" Travis asked, playing with a strand of her hair.

"Well, only if you want to," Claire hedged.

"Oh, I want to. In fact, if we leave right now, we could be back before it's time to go to my parents' house. They will be ecstatic because they have a new daughter-in-law."

Claire kissed him and then listened while Travis put a call into the airport and scheduled their flight.

When he hung up, he asked her, "An Elvis impersonator. Are you sure about that?"

"Positive." Claire smiled at him. "Life is short, and I want to spend whatever time we have left making memories. I can't imagine finding another man who could possibly understand me more than you do."

Travis skimmed his hand down her cheek and then kissed her on the nose before taking her lips in a kiss filled with passion and an intensity that he'd held back before. "I can't think of anything I would like more. Will you go with me when I travel to our other stores and help get the childcare centers going there?"

"What about the Chicago director's position?"

"We'll find a replacement. Somebody who can handle the stress and truly loves working with children."

Claire grinned at him, "So, when do we leave?"

"Two hours. Do you want a dress?"

"Do I need one?"

"It's customary."

"What about the gold dress I wore for the Christmas party? Will that work?"

"You know it will. Go get dressed, and I'll do the same. We'll celebrate on the way there and then again when we get back."

Claire hurried to the borrowed bedroom and quickly donned the gold dress. She re-did her makeup and then decided to take down her ponytail and brush her hair.

"Ready to go?" Travis asked from the doorway.

"Yes," Claire nodded and joined him.

This is my life. Take Two.

Epilogue

Guardian Angel School

Hope was very happy with how things were working out for both Claire and Travis. They'd just decided to get married, and while they were headed to Las Vegas, Hope wasn't following them. She hated everything about the city and had decided she would position herself so that she could render quick help if needed, but she wouldn't have to be bombarded by the depravity of humanity that filled the city streets.

She headed for the school rooms, hoping she could find Matthias, but instead she found Theo there. He gave her a quick assessing look and then waved her forward.

"Little angel, what can I do for you?"

"I'm looking for Matthias."

"He'll be back shortly. You can wait here for him if you like."

"Thank you."

"So, how goes your assignment?" Theo asked.

"Very good. I believe I've done what I was sent for. Travis and Claire and going to be married tomorrow in Las Vegas."

"From your joyful expression, I'm guessing this is a good turn of events?"

"Yes, most definitely. Both of them have dealt with their past grief and opened their hearts to a second-chance love. It was neat to watch it unfold."

"You talk as if you had nothing to do with it?"

Hope shrugged her shoulders. "In truth, I'm not sure I did.

209

At least, not these last few days. Travis and Claire were able to navigate things mostly on their own."

"Well, that's one way to ensure you didn't break any rules."

"Yes. I learned my lesson last year."

"I hear your charges are getting married?" Matthias asked, as he arrived in the school room.

"Yes. Claire wants to get married by Elvis…"

Theo and Matthias shared a look and Matthias shook his head. "I'm afraid that is not at all possible."

"I know that. I was just making conversation. Anyway, I was hoping to find Joy and Charity up here. I wondered how things were going with their charges."

"Joy was here earlier, and she reported that true love had won the day. Her charges are getting married as well."

"So, everything worked out well. I'm so glad."

"Nothing like a little Christmas magic to be concerned about."

"So, do you want to continue with the same charges you've been working on?"

"Oh, I want to stay with Travis and Claire. Their future looks very right."

"Merry Christmas, Hope. Now and every day of the year."

Hope nodded, then slipped back down to where Travis and Claire had just finished exchanging their vows. They kissed and made short work of signing the marriage license.

"Now what?" Claire asked.

"Now, we go home and see if that happily ever after is waiting just around the corner."

Hope smiled at Travis' words. "I'll do my best to make sure you have a happy existence. Within reason. Don't ask for things I can't give you."

Hope watched Travis lead Claire back to the rented limo, giving instructions for it to return to the airport. The couple was obviously enthralled with one another. They gave the sights and sounds of Las Vegas no attention whatsoever. Second chance love had found them, and in the process, their hearts had begun to heal. That was the greatest miracle in their lives, spurred by the greatest miracle of all—Love.

Sample Story

<u>Christmas Angel Joy, Three Christmas Angels Book One</u>

Prologue

Guardian Angel School

Heaven

"Hallelujah! Amen!"

The sound of the voices faded away as everyone paused, serene smiles upon their faces.

"Very nice. Let's all take a few moments to ourselves before the celebration starts. Polish your halos. Fluff your wings. Practice your smiles." The choirmaster smiled at them before leaving the room.

Matthias watched as the angels that were part of the angelic chorus departed the choir room, and then he frowned as three little white robed angels snuck out the side door. He was debating about following them when a voice spoke from behind him.

"I wouldn't waste any time going after them. Those three look like they're up to something. I thought this was supposed to be a celebration and yet, they look as if they are preparing for a funeral mass."

Matthias turned and nodded his head, "I was just thinking that same thing. I was hoping to have a quiet Christmas season, but with those three…"

"…there is no such thing as *quiet*."

Matthias nodded and then sighed before heading for the same door where the trio had made their escape. Alexander, the angel in charge of the guard, chuckled and then headed for the courtyard and his post for the rest of the day's celebration. Rather than celebrating Christmas on December 25th only, Heaven celebrated for the entire month. Matthias looked forward to partaking in today's celebration, but first, he had three wayward angels to round up.

He watched the last of the trio slip around the hedge at the back of the school. Pausing beside a fountain on the other side of the courtyard, he kept his distance for the moment but made sure he had a clear view of them, as they entered the building. Each of them took a seat at a small table, one dropping her head into her hands while the other two looked both morose and hopeless.

Hopeless? Guardian angels weren't allowed to look hopeless. No angels were allowed to ever look hopeless. There was no such thing within the Heavenly realms. Angels were supposed to inspire, bring about hope, and encourage humans to have faith; never give up or wallow in despair.

Sighing, Matthias stood to his full height and moved in their direction. It was time to fulfill his responsibilities. He was in charge of training the newer guardian angels. He entered the small schoolroom and then stopped a few feet away from the three.

"What are you three angels doing?" Matthias asked. "The celebration is about to begin."

When none of them offered an answer to his question, he crossed his arms over his chest and made a noise letting them know his patience wasn't everlasting.

Young angels in training could be considered quite troublesome by some of the older angels, but Matthias had willingly embraced taking the youngsters under his wings and helping them become the very best guardian angels they could be. This was his second year supervising this particular trio of angels. He knew better than to let them congregate and share their woes with one another. In the past, that had led to them giving one another advice, most of which violated the angel code and had forced him to intervene and correct the resulting situations. He did not look forward to repeating those experiences this Christmas season.

He cleared his throat to gain their attention and then met their eyes, one by one. "Well?"

"My little boy is so sad," Joy told him, dramatically tossing her hands out to her sides.

Joy was just beginning her second year of guardian angel training. She had struggled with several of her assignments in the past twelve months. In order to graduate from the guardian angel school, the little angels were given a variety of special assignments. All three of these angels had failed their special assignments the year before and were being given another chance to fulfill their duties without interfering in ways that were off-limits.

Humans were complex creatures with a God-given free will. While the angels could help facilitate opportunities, they weren't allowed to force or coerce their charges to do the prudent and correct thing. Joy had forgotten that fact the year before when she had played upon her charge's emotions in order to get them to follow a certain path. Unfortunately for Joy, human emotions were very volatile. Soon enough, her charge realized she had been manipulated but had blamed that fact upon a close family member, not where the blame had truly belonged—on her guardian angel.

Matthias had removed Joy from her guardianship of that human and had spent the next two months helping to bring about a reconciliation between the two humans; all because of the misconception that had arisen by Joy's overstep. Explaining the situation to the Archangel who oversaw the entire guardian angel program had been even worse. Matthias never wanted to go through that experience again.

Matthias nodded in acknowledgement of her response and then looked to the next angel. "And you, Hope? The last time we talked you were excited about your current assignment."

"My charge doesn't even want to celebrate Christmas this year," Hope stated, huffing out a breath, as she dropped her chin into her cupped hands. "How can anyone not want to celebrate Christmas? It's not…well, it's just not right. Or human. They love Christmas and their made-up celebratory figures. The snowman who danced and sang…"

"…and then melted when the sun came out," Matthias told her with a small smile.

"I'm talking about before that. And humans love the story of the little reindeer whose nose glowed and could fly. That story had a happy ending."

"But the idea behind Christmas has nothing to do with those things," Matthias reminded her needlessly.

"I know that." Hope nodded and added, "But my charge's file states that she loved all of those things until a year ago. Now, she abhors the very idea of Christmas. I'm trying not to hold that against her, but I must confess; it's very hard. Christmas is the most wonderful time of the year, but my charge hates it."

"Well, at least your charge doesn't visit the cemetery every day. It's really sad to watch her cry—day after day—and not even try to go on living her life," Charity added.

Charity was the most mature of the angels in training and had already successfully completed two of the three special assignments. If she was successful in helping her current charge overcome a soul-searing grief, she would graduate at the end of January.

Matthias looked at the three and shook his head, "So you three are just going to sit around up here moaning about your difficult situations rather than try to find a solution to them?"

Joy looked up at him. "What are we supposed to do? I mean, it's only a few weeks before Christmas. How are people supposed to remember they're celebrating the birth of the Christ Child if they are so unhappy?"

Matthias grinned. "You find a way to make them happy. Help them remember the good things in life and give them hope which is what Christmas is all about. Your job is to try to get your charges to see that. Remember…a guardian angel doesn't just keep their charge from getting run over as they cross the street; you also have to help your charge in the emotional, spiritual, and mental realm."

The three angels looked at each other. Their expressions slowly started to change. Hope was the first to speak.

"I could help Claire want to celebrate Christmas."

"And I could help Maddie find another outlet for her grief," added Charity. "What about you, Joy? Why is your little boy so sad?"

Joy was happy that her friends were coming up with solutions. Maybe they could help her brainstorm a solution to her little charge's request. While the other two angels had been assigned adult charges, Joy had been assigned to watch over a little boy. She'd considered herself the luckiest of the three when they'd been given their assignments. Now, she wasn't so sure. "My little boy wants his mama not to be so sad. She's lonely. He wants to help her but doesn't know how."

"Maybe she needs a puppy to love?" Hope suggested with a smile.

"Puppies are nice. So are kittens," Charity offered. "This

216

time of year, there are always an abundance at the animal shelters. Maybe your little charge's mother could adopt a new pet?"

Joy appreciated their help, but she didn't think either of their answers were going to help Sam, her charge. Puppies and kittens took a lot of energy. After watching them, Sam's mother lacked extra energy at this time.

Matthias squatted down so that he was eye-level with the littlest of the three angels. "You'll find a way. I have faith in you."

"Thanks?" Joy queried, wishing she had as much faith in herself, as the head of the angel school seemed to have. "Maybe we should brainstorm more ideas…"

Matthias shook his head, "That is not going to happen while I'm around. I'm still recovering from the last brainstorming session you three had together. If you need to bounce ideas off of someone, I am always available to you."

Joy gave him a sheepish look and then snuck a glance at her two companions, noticing that they also looked embarrassed and were trying to avoid Matthias' searing glance. She decided it was up to her to put Matthias in a better mood. She offered him a small smile. "I guess I should probably get back down there, huh?"

"That would be a good place to start," Matthias agreed with a nod and warm smile. "You should all be busy trying to help your charges right now. Christmas is only two weeks away. You all should know better than anyone just how fast time can fly. Go and tend to your charges and remember; I am always here if you need advice or just to talk through a plan."

Hope, Charity and Joy nodded dutifully, and each said, "Thank you."

Matthias smiled at each of them. "Off with you all now. Go enjoy the celebration for a bit and then take that enthusiasm back to your duties. We'll have even more to celebrate once you three have your charges sorted out."

Joy looked at her friends. They all silently agreed. They were going to help their charges, whether those charges wanted to be helped right now or not. Their charges would never know why their situations had changed. The angels would have to comply with the rules and regulations for interactions with their humans. They would need to keep in mind; where there was a will, there was always a way.

Joy smiled and said, "I'm heading down there right now. Thanks, Matthias."

"What about the celebration?" Hope asked her, glancing out the window of the schoolroom to see the other angels gathering around the center of the courtyard. The choir performance was about to start.

Joy shook her head, smiling brightly as she replied, "There's so much to be thankful for and happy about this time of year. I don't need a celebration to remind me of that. I just need to figure out how to make Sam's dream come true. Then, everything will work out just fine."

Matthias smiled approvingly at her. "Good luck to you, Joy. I look forward to hearing a good report from you. Charity and Hope, good luck to you as well. The miracles of Christmas are just beginning."

Chapter 1

Two weeks before Christmas

Denver, Colorado

"Bye, Mrs. O'Toole," Sam waved as he skipped off the school bus.

"You go right up to your mother's office, Sam," the smiling bus driver told him.

"I will. I promise." Sam struggled for a moment to put his arms through his backpack straps. After a little hop, it settled into place. His winter hat had shifted only slightly atop his head of wheat-colored curls.

He rushed headlong for the double glass doors, not even breaking his stride when the security guard, Jim, saw him coming and held the door open.

"Good afternoon, Sam."

"Hi, Mr. Jim. I'm in a hurry."

"I can see that. Have a good afternoon."

"I will," Sam yelled back.

He started for the bank of elevators, only to shake his head at the crowd already waiting for their turn in the foyer. He veered to his left, pushed through the door to the stairwell, and ran up the stairs until he reached the third-floor landing. He pulled open the heavy door that was stamped with a big red three. Sighing with relief, his feet hurried over the carpeted hallway as he headed for the office at the end.

Sam rushed into the office that had City of Denver, Planning and Events Division stenciled on the door. As always, his mother sat her desk. Sam was oblivious to the presence of his guardian angel, hovering just behind him, as she kept watch over her young charge. He was slightly out of breath, but that didn't dampen his enthusiasm one bit.

"Mom. I'm here. Can we go to the park now?" He wiggled his arms and allowed his backpack to drop with a dull thud to the floor.

Melissa Bartell looked up from the paper she'd been studying and forced a smile to her lips.

"Hey, little man. How was school?" She opened her arms and the little boy rushed into them, hugged her briefly and then danced away again, unable to stay still for even a few seconds.

"School was good. Can we go now?" Sam asked, hopping from foot to foot and twirling toward the large windows in the office that overlooked the city below.

"You saw that it was snowing outside, right?" Melissa asked, as she got up from her desk and joined her son at the windows. When her cell phone beeped, reminding her that she was running late for a meeting, she reached for the coat she'd discarded an hour earlier. "Sure you want to go hang out in a city park covered in snow instead of at home where it's nice and warm?"

"Yeah." Sam rolled his eyes at the same time he nodded his head while adding, "I have my hat and my gloves." He held up the gloves and then waved his stocking hat in the air for her to see.

Melissa tousled his hair and then smiled down at him. "Okay, I guess I can stress while walking through the park as well as I can stress sitting here. Let's go."

Sam frowned at his mother's comments and Joy leaned closer, wondering what was bothering the beautiful young mother. It was easy to see where Sam got his coloring from, his mother's long blonde tresses had streaks of gold and a blonde that was so light it was a shimmery white mixed throughout. Her gray eyes matched Sam's, as did the small dimple that appeared in her cheek as it did in Sam's whenever he was happy and smiling; behaviors that happened far too seldom in recent days for Joy's liking.

"Why are you stressing?" Sam asked, taking his mother's gloved hand, as they left her office and took the elevator down to the ground floor. His mother nodded at Jim as they exited the building and began the short walk to the city park. There was a slight breeze, but Sam didn't even feel the cold. He was waiting on his mother for an answer to his question.

Melissa glanced down at him and made a silly face, "It's been a bad—very bad—day."

Sam pursed his lips at her reference to one of his favorite books; *Alexander and the Terrible, Horrible, No Good, Very Bad Day.*

He highly doubted his mother was capable of having such a day, but then again, being an adult seemed like lots of work and very little fun. He stepped a little closer to her and then nodded and pursed his lips in a bad imitation of the look she always gave him in such a situation. "So, tell me all about it."

Melissa chuckled and shook her head at his silliness. "Where have I heard that before?"

"You. It's what you always tell me when I've had a bad day. I'm all ears, mom."

Melissa shook her head again and laid a hand on his jacketed shoulder, "Thanks, sweetie, but you don't need to worry about my problems."

"Mom! You always say we're a team of two." Sam danced away from her and turned around so that he was walking backwards and threw his arms out to the side. "You talk and I'll listen."

Melissa raised a brow at her son and then spun him around, so he wouldn't stumble and fall into the street. "I've heard that before, as well." She winked at him and then explained the most pressing issue on her mind. "So, I got a phone call earlier this afternoon. It seems there was an accident and the Christmas trees aren't coming," she told him, keeping her eyes straight ahead. She tried to push aside the panic saying the words aloud had created.

A Christmas Festival without Christmas trees? Who had ever heard of such a thing? If the festival wasn't a success this year... People from all over the Denver area come to visit the festival with the intention of purchasing their Christmas tree at the end of the outing. Once word gets out that there are no Christmas trees this year, will anyone even bother to drive across town?

Sam stopped walking, pulling on his mother's hand to gain her attention. "The Christmas trees aren't coming? But...but the Christmas trees...you can't have a Christmas festival without Christmas trees."

Melissa nodded sadly and squatted down, so she was on eye-level with Sam. "I agree, buddy. However, this close to Christmas, there's not enough time to find another supplier to haul them out here. Besides, the two Christmas tree farms I called this afternoon don't have enough trees or manpower to harvest the trees they have left. I don't know what I'm going to do. I've kind of exhausted my available options."

Sam nodded, as Melissa stood back up, and they continued walking. His little expression was still far too serious, as they entered the park. Almost immediately, his mother was snagged by a vendor who had questions. Sam knew it would be quite a while before his mother made her way to the center tent and impatience won out.

"I'm going to the nativity scene, mom," Sam called out even as he was walking away.

"Sam, stay where I can see you. Okay?" Melissa called out after him. The nativity scene was just a few dozen yards away from the event tent and easily seen from their present location.

"I will." Sam waved and took off, making sure he walked through the fresh snow and left his mark upon the landscape.

The city park where the festival was being held sat between the Museum of Natural History and the Denver Zoo. It was a large property and included a small golf course which was now closed due to the inclement weather. Melissa was only utilizing one small corner of the park for the Christmas Festival. In the distance, one could see the warning fence that had been erected to keep festival attendees from wandering onto the golf course.

The year before, a group of teenagers had wandered onto the golf course during the Christmas Festival and had vandalized the caddy shack before anyone had realized what was happening. The damages had been small, but the city manager had blamed Melissa for not having foreseen that such a thing might happen. Melissa had assured him that additional precautions would be taken this year. She could only cross her fingers as the opening of the festival neared and pray that they wouldn't have any incidences. Too much was riding on the festival being successful this year.

Melissa finally broke free from the vendors and headed for her makeshift headquarters here at City Park. Several large pressurized domes had already been set up where vendors could sell their wares and where she and her staff would oversee and manage the festival. Hot air kept the domes inflated and also warmed the air inside, making them a pleasant escape from the chilly weather outside. This was a new amenity being offered this year. Melissa was hopeful it would bring more people out in attendance.

Her assistant met her with a stack of messages. Melissa inwardly cringed when she saw more than half of them were from the last man she wanted to deal with today. The city manager. She

223

tucked the messages from him to the back of the pile, ignoring the knowing smile her assistant sent her way, and then headed for her makeshift desk. With any luck, she wouldn't have any more problems heaped on her shoulders. She needed a chance to figure out the tree situation and several other pressing concerns before she could handle even one more issue.

***

Sam reached the nativity scene and quickly slipped over the railing and sat down by the manger. This is where he'd been coming for the last week and, like those other times, he began speaking to the fake infant, telling it all about his mother's unhappiness and how he didn't need anything for Christmas; he just wanted his mother to be happy.

"Baby Jesus, Christmas is only a few weeks away. I don't need anything for myself, but please bring mama a husband. Maybe if she wasn't so lonely, she'd be happy again. I looked at school today, but I didn't find anyone who didn't already have a mama and a daddy. It makes mama sad when she comes to my school plays. She has to sit all by herself."

Sam grew quiet for a moment and then he added another request. "Mama's real sad about the Christmas trees. Could you maybe send her some of them, too? My friends all went and talked to the guy in the Santa suit at the mall, but I told them that was just silly. Mrs. Barnes taught us in Sunday school that Jesus has all the answers to our problems. That's why I'm talking to You about this."

He looked up at the winter sky and then glanced back at the plastic baby. "I know there's lots of people in the world with big problems, but maybe…if it's not too much to ask, you could answer mine?"

"Sam!" his mother's voice carried over the crisp air.

"I gotta go, but I'll be back tomorrow. Thanks for helping

224

my mama." Sam got to his feet and climbed over the railing. He waved to his mother and rushed to where she was patiently waiting. When he reached her side, he announced, "I'm hungry." side.

She chuckled and nodded. "Tell me something new. How about we stop and grab a pizza before heading home?"

"Yes!" Sam agreed, as he raised a fist in the air. Pizza was his all-time favorite food.

***

Joy watched as mother and son headed for her vehicle, parked only a block away. A plan was already beginning to form for how to deal with Sam's unhappiness and his latest request. This was the first time Sam had actually mentioned what he thought might make his mama happy. A husband.

That immediately got Joy thinking. She was almost giddy at the idea of playing matchmaker. She'd have to follow the rules, which meant she couldn't toy with anyone's emotions. After last year's debacle, she'd promised Matthias to stick to the guardian angel code, but making sure Melissa Bartell had an opportunity to meet an eligible man wasn't in that book of codes. Melissa hadn't know that she should've been dreaming about a certain eligible man all these months.

Joy had been watching the request board which angels used to help one another do their jobs more efficiently. Just yesterday, a fellow angel had posted about her charge who was discouraged because he hadn't been able to find a buyer for his trees. The man had started his own Christmas tree farm a number of years earlier and was finally ready to start selling them, but a series of events had prevented him from harvesting them earlier. Now, he couldn't find anyone nearby to purchase them. The man's location was less than two hours away from Denver. To Joy, this situation was tailor-made in heaven. She wasn't about to let this opportunity slip away.

225

Joy immediately sent out a request and headed off to meet the other angel. To set things in motion, she needed a business card to fall into Sam's mom's hands. With the Christmas tree situation taken care of, now she only needed to find Sam's mom a husband. Compared to some of the other tasks she'd performed, this one should be a piece of cake...make that a Christmas yule log. It was the holiday season, after all.

Chapter 2

Two days later…

"Melissa, the guy from the tree farm is here," Sandy James called up the ladder to where her boss—the person in charge of making the Christmas Festival a success—was currently trying to untangle a string of lights. Why one of the city maintenance workers wasn't up on the ladder was unclear at the moment.

"Just a minute," a voice answered back, as the ladder started wobbling dangerously.

"Whoa!" Sandy lunged forward to stabilize the ladder just as another body pushed her out of the way and grabbed the ladder with big hands.

"I've got this," a deep tenor voice floated up to the top of the ladder. Melissa looked down into the bluest eyes she'd ever seen. "You okay up there?"

Melissa nodded and then blushed when she remembered he could only see the lower half of her since her head was partially concealed behind the festival's sign. Taking a calming breath, she called back down, "I'm fine. I'm coming down right now."

She descended the ladder, pausing when she reached the point where the stranger was holding it steady.

"Thank you," she murmured, as he stepped back, so she climbed the rest of the way down. She dusted off her hands and then looked past the stranger to where Sandy stood patiently waiting. She looked to Sandy's right and then gave the stranger a cursory glance. She wasn't sure who he was, but he was handsome, dressed in a red plaid flannel jacket with a hoodie pulled up over his hair. She briefly wondered what his hair looked like, but she quickly dismissed her wayward thoughts, bringing them back to the present. She didn't have time in her life for anything more than a fleeting second of appreciation for a handsome man—and this man definitely fit that category.

He appeared to be giving her appearance a thorough once-over as well. Melissa met his eyes briefly once more and then turned away, as she felt a blush creep into her cheeks. She didn't have time for…whatever, this was. There was no denying the man was gorgeous and exactly the type of man Melissa would be attracted to, if she ever gave herself permission to go down that road again. She currently didn't have time or the inclination for any sort of relationship if it didn't involve work and the festival. She most definitely didn't have time to nurse a broken heart. In her experience, heartbreak was the only thing at the end of the road when dealing with a handsome man. No, thank you.

She looked back at Sandy with a raised brow, "You said the guy from the tree farm was here. Where is he?"

She'd only spoken to the man on the phone a few times. She'd been expecting an older gentleman, possibly with greying or even white hair. His voice had been gravelly, and she'd pictured a slimmer version of Santa. Her imagination had placed him sitting in a rocking chair with a pipe in one hand, as he talked to her about his Christmas trees on the phone with the other. She didn't see anyone fitting that description nearby.

Sandy bit her bottom lip and then pointed unobtrusively at the stranger. Melissa turned her head and made eye contact with the handsome man. He nodded and stuck out his hand. She took it, ignoring how warm it was and how strong it felt.

"I would be the guy with the Christmas trees."

She ignored the way his deep blue eyes seemed to sparkle with mirth and forced herself to act professional. "Sorry. I'm Melissa Bartell, Community Events Director, and this is my assistant Sandy James. I was expecting…" She broke off, as she realized how rude her assumptions might seem if she were to give voice to them.

"Sandy and I already met," his deep voice reverberated inside her chest, and a feeling of warmth surrounded her. He shook her hand and the feeling of warmth flowed up her arm. "Jarod Gregory. Christmas Valley Pines." He looked around and then offered her a smile. "This is no small undertaking you have going on here."

Melissa smiled back, his comment helping her focus on the reason he was standing before her. "This is my fifth year running the festival. Each year, it seems to get more complicated than the last. Before I forget, thank you so much for stepping in at the last minute. The Christmas tree supplier we've used for the last few years hit a patch of ice coming through Idaho and their trailer overturned."

Jarod looked concerned. "Was anyone injured?"

"Only the four hundred trees he was carrying. Actually, I spoke to him a few days ago. He said quite a few of the trees remained undamaged, but his tractor trailer didn't fare as well. With it being so close to the holidays, he couldn't find another way to transport the trees out here until the twentieth of December which is a few days before the festival ends."

"Without the draw of the Christmas trees, we wouldn't get nearly as many people to attend the festival," Sandy interjected, moving forward into their small circle. "The city council is looking for ways to save money. This festival has been on their hatchet list for the last two years. If attendance was to suddenly drop, they would cut us out of next year's budget in a heartbeat."

Jarod nodded his understanding and then looked around for a moment before turning back to the conversation. "Well, I'm happy I could help."

"Let's go this way, and I'll show you what we have designated for the tree lot," Melissa told him, turning and walking toward the opposite side of the area cordoned off for the festival.

"This is actually the first year I've had trees to sell," Jarod informed her, "I inherited the land from my grandfather and moved out here from Oregon almost seven years ago now. My parents have a big tree farm back there and provided me the seedlings needed to start one here, but it takes years before a new operation is ready to do more than tend the trees." Jarod walked by her side, his long legs eating up the distance, but he walked at a leisurely pace, so Melissa was impressed that she never once felt as if she was having to hurry to keep up with him.

Melissa veered to her right and they began to cut across the center of the park. "Seven years is a long time to do nothing but watch trees grow. I had to admit I was actually shocked to find that there was someone in that area of the state who was growing trees. The pine beetles have all but decimated the national forests around here."

Jarod made a sound of agreement. "I noticed that when I first came out here. We have the same thing back in Oregon, so I was prepared for how to protect my farm. I spray the trees in early May and then make sure they're getting enough fertilizer and water throughout the growing season. Healthy trees don't seem to be the beetle's natural habitat, so I do my best to make sure mine are the healthiest in the county. So far, I haven't had any trees get infected."

"Well, I hope you don't. Let me show you where you'll be setting up. There's already a fence around the area with lights and such."

Melissa led him past the life-sized nativity scene, halting her forward progress when she spied her son inside the scene, kneeling next to the manger and the figure of baby Jesus. She saw his lips move, as he carried on a one-sided conversation with the infant and sighed. Sam had seemed so down this holiday Season, and he'd been insistent on coming to the park with her each afternoon when school was out. He didn't seem interested in the exhibits being set up, except for one; the nativity scene.

Jarod nodded his head toward Sam and asked, "Someone you know?"

"My son," she told him with a small turn of her lips.

"He seems to be having quite the conversation over there," Jarod pointed out.

Melissa nodded, "A daily occurrence, I assure you." She stepped forward and called out, "Sam."

Her son turned his head and then waved. She waved back and gestured for him to join her, smiling when he picked up his backpack and ran to her. She bent down and hugged him when he got there, "Hey. I thought maybe you'd like to go see the Christmas trees."

Sam's eyes widened, and he looked at Jarod, "Did he bring them?"

Melissa nodded, "He did. On a big truck?" she guessed, looking to Jarod for confirmation.

"On a big truck. You look like you're pretty smart. You interested in helping me out for a little bit?" Jarod asked, earning a grin from Sam and a curious look from Melissa.

"What kind of help are we talking about?" Melissa asked.

"Well, I need to keep track of the trees as they're unloaded. I brought a couple of high school guys with me to get the stands on and everything unloaded, but I could sure use someone to help keep track of things. You can count, can't you?" Jarod asked with a smirk he barely managed to contain.

Sam stood up tall and nodded, "I can count really high. My

teacher says I'm excst...excert...."

He looked at Melissa, and she provided the word he was looking for, "Exceptional."

Sam grinned, "Yeah. Exceptional. I'm exceptional at math."

"Great. You're the man I need."

Melissa shook her head as Sam took off sprinting across the snow-covered expanse of lawn, "I hope you know what you just signed up for."

"I have two nephews and three nieces," Jarod informed her. "I've missed them, and Sam seems like a great kid."

Melissa nodded, "He is."

They reached the fenced space, and she asked, "What do you think? Will this be enough room?"

Jarod looked around and then nodded. "Plenty. I'd better get things rolling here, so we can get unloaded before dark. Your assistant mentioned something about the festival opening a day early?"

Melissa gave him an apologetic look, "Yeah. Sorry I didn't have a chance to let you know. They're forecasting a big storm tomorrow and most of the vendors are ready to go so we're doing a soft open tonight. We'll open at six o'clock. Any chance you might be ready to sell trees by then? So many people wait to purchase their Christmas tree from the lot here...there'll be a lot of disappointed people if they have to go somewhere else."

Sam came running back to them, a giddy smile spread across his little face. "Mom! You should see all of the trees. Oodles and oodles of them."

"I hope so, we have oodles and oodles of people coming to buy them. About tonight?" she asked Jarod hesitantly.

"We'll be ready. After all, I have an exceptional counter ready to help out."

Jarod bumped gloved knuckles with Sam. She felt a pain in her heart. She'd married his father right out of college and had thought they were on the same page where their family was concerned. Sam's dad had left almost immediately after Melissa had told him he was going to be a father. He'd told her he wasn't ready to be tied down to a kid and, when she'd refused to even consider an abortion, he'd filed for a quick divorce and moved to California.

Melissa had been so excited about the prospect of becoming a mom, she hadn't even thought about fighting Tyler over the divorce or asking for child support. He'd made it clear he wanted nothing to do with his child. Melissa had petitioned the court to go back to using her maiden name. She'd given it to Sam when he was born and listed his father on the birth certificate, but that had been where Tyler Jamison's connection to her son ended.

As Sam had gotten older, she'd been struggling with a sense of guilt that he didn't have a man in his life to help guide him through the coming years. Sam was in second grade now. He was also the only child in his class that didn't have at least one father figure in his life. Her own parents were no longer around to help out. It was just her and Sam.

Some days, it was all she could do to get through the day by telling herself that tomorrow would be better. Tomorrow, she wouldn't feel lonely. Tomorrow, she'd find someone to confide in that didn't wear *Teenage Mutant Ninja Turtle* pajamas to bed. Tomorrow…

"Mom?" Sam was tugging on the hem of her coat.

"What?" she looked down and realized she'd let her mind drift. "Oh, Sam. I'm sorry. Lots of things on my mind this time of year. Are you okay sticking around and helping Mr. Gregory with the trees?"

"Sure. I count things really good."

"I know you do," she touched his shoulder for a brief moment and then took a step back. "I'll let you boys get to it, then. Sam, I'll be over at the event tent. When you're done helping Mr. Gregory, you come find me. Okay?"

"Okay," Sam readily agreed, dismissing her and starting up a conversation with Jarod right away.

Melissa watched for a long moment, pushing aside the guilt and unhappiness that always crept in whenever she thought of her fatherless son. She was doing the best she could, but the holidays were always hard. On both of them.

As she headed back to tackle the next item on her to-do list, she made a mental note to check out the local Boys and Girls Club right after the first of the year. Sam needed a male role model in his life. She'd heard from several people about the Big Brother program and how well it was doing. She couldn't make Sam's dad acknowledge his existence, but maybe she could find someone who would pay attention to Sam and help him grow into a fine young man. Someone who might be willing to teach him what being a real man was all about and answer the questions she knew he would have in the future but might not feel comfortable talking to her about.

"Sandy," she called out, as she entered the tent. "Did this evening's entertainment show up yet?"

"They just arrived."

Melissa nodded, glad that the local rock band had been willing and able to fill the stage on a moment's notice. They were popular amongst the younger population, and she was hoping that would draw a younger demographic out to the festival. "Anything else pressing right now?"

"You and a cup of hot chocolate," Sandy informed her, handing her a covered cup and turning her toward her makeshift office. "Go kick your feet up for five minutes."

"But...," Melissa took the cup and a few steps forward, but then she remembered the list of items she still needed to deal with.

"I promise none of your problems are going to go away in the next five minutes." Sandy gave her a look with one raised brow, daring her to argue. "You know I'm right."

"As always. Fine, but only for five minutes." She took the hot chocolate, sipping it as she sat down and leaned back in the chair. She tried to clear her brain, but that only allowed the image of the Christmas tree man to intrude. He was handsome...but, she couldn't allow herself to be swayed by that. Nor could she spend time wondering why walking beside him had felt so...right.

Had I ever felt like that with Sam's dad?

Realizing where her thoughts were headed, she sat up and pushed the unfinished cup of hot chocolate away. No, she had a job to do. It was time to focus on the festival now. The past wasn't something she would change. The present day demanded she do her best to ensure the thousands of people who would be arriving later today had a memorable experience. Her personal problems would just have to wait.

Thank You

Dear Reader,

Thank you for choosing to read my books out of the thousands that merit reading. I recognize that reading takes time and quietness, so I am grateful that you have designed your lives to allow for this enriching endeavor, whatever the book's title and subject.

Now more than ever before, Amazon reviews and Social Media play vital role in helping individuals make their reading choices. If any of my books have moved you, inspired you, or educated you, please share your reactions with others by posting an Amazon review as well as via email, Facebook, Twitter, Goodreads, -- or even old-fashioned face-to-face conversation! And when you receive my announcement of my new book, please pass it along. Thank you.

For updates about New Releases, as well as exclusive promotions, visit my website and sign up for the VIP mailing list. Click here to get started: www.morrisfenrisbooks.com

I invite you to visit my Facebook page often facebook.com/AuthorMorrisFenris where I post not only my news, but announcements of other authors' work.

For my portfolio of books on Amazon, please visit my Author Page:

Amazon USA:
amazon.com/author/morrisfenris

Amazon UK:
https://www.amazon.co.uk/Morris%20Fenris/e/B00FXLWKRC

You can also contact me by email:
authormorrisfenris@gmail.com

With profound gratitude, and with hope for your continued reading pleasure,

Morris Fenris
Author & Publisher

Made in the USA
Columbia, SC
13 November 2020

24425582R00143